OREGON DISASTER

RACHEL WESSON

LONDONGATE PUBLISHING

Copyright © 2017 by Rachel Wesson. This edition revised May 2024.

All rights reserved.

No part of this book may be reproduced in any form or by any electronic or mechanical means, including information storage and retrieval systems, without written permission from the author, except for the use of brief quotations in a book review.

PROLOGUE

PORTLAND, OREGON

Sarah tossed and turned before deciding to give up on sleep. She still couldn't believe her pa and ma had said no. Edwin had been right. They should have just eloped and not bothered to ask permission. Well, tonight she would leave and never come back. She wasn't going to wait a year to marry. She loved Edwin, and he loved her. She closed her eyes, imagining the feel of his lips on hers. He generated feelings in her body she didn't fully understand. But she knew enough not to do everything he wanted. He would have to wait until they were married. She wondered if his home was as nice as he said it was. Not that she thought he was lying, but men's ideas of comfortable weren't quite the same as women's. Still, she would be in charge of her own home. She could make Edwin wonderful meals and have them ready when he came in from a hard day's work. Then, when he struck it rich, he would buy her the biggest house anyone had seen. They would have servants and she would live a life of leisure. She wrapped her arms around herself. In a few hours, she would leave Portland with Edwin. She wouldn't look back.

First, though, she had to tell her parents. They weren't really her parents. Uncle Rick had taken her and her sister Carrie in when their ma died on the Oregon trail. Then he married Jo and they had all lived together since.

She picked up the pen, dipped it in the ink, and scribbled a quick note. It wasn't right, so she tore it up and started again. An owl hooted outside the window, reminding her she didn't have much time. Edwin had said he would be waiting in the orchard for her at two in the morning. Everyone would be asleep by then. She was going to leave without saying anything, but she couldn't do that.

Dear Pa, Ma, and Carrie,

I love Edwin and want to marry him now and not in a year's time. We are eloping. By the time you get this, we will have married. Please don't come after us. I know you think we are too young and Edwin is not the man I believe him to be, but you are wrong on both counts. I am 18–older than Jo was when she met you, Uncle Rick.

We will be back one day when Edwin has struck it rich. In the meantime, take care.

Love, Sarah. x

She read it again. Would Rick and Jo even notice she had gone? Would they care? They were too busy worrying about Almanzo. Not to mention the two missing girls who were complete strangers. She came very low on their list of priorities. They knew how much she loved Edwin. She had tried to do the right thing by persuading Edwin to come and speak to Pa. But Rick had been too stubborn. As if she was going to wait a year before she could get married.

She tore the letter to shreds. Edwin was right. Her uncle Rick and Jo may claim to be her ma and pa, but they didn't love her or Carrie. Uncle Rick was going to abandon them at an orphanage until Jo stopped him. Sarah bit her lip. That was years ago, though. They had children of their own now. Edwin said the six-year-old twins would always come first in Rick and Johanna's eyes. She hadn't noticed them treating her and Carrie differently, but then, maybe she was blind. Edwin said she was innocent about many things.

She looked to Carrie's bedroom across the hall. She imagined Carrie was snoring softly. She would miss her sister and wished they hadn't argued that afternoon. Worried about Almanzo, Carrie had wondered aloud how the two missing girls would be. Sarah's face still stung from where Carrie had hit her. She hadn't meant to be nasty, but Edwin was right. Who would want to marry two white girls who had been living with Indians for almost a week? If they weren't already dead, Sarah guessed they wished they were. Carrie had slapped her across the face. Her sister reminded her the Indians could be nice ones like Paco, Walking Tall and his tribe. Not that Edwin believed there was such a thing as a nice Indian. Carrie had taken the Indian's side over hers. She'd even said she hated Edwin. Her little sister was going to be sorry. She wouldn't say anything to her about leaving. Picking up the pen, she dipped it into the ink before writing,

To Rick and Jo, I love Edwin. We will be married by the time you read this. Please do not follow us. Goodbye. Sarah.

With one last look around her room, Sarah picked up her carpet bag and opened the door. Sarah held her breath until she was outside the house. Nobody had woken. Part of her wished they had. Then they may see she was serious and let her stay and marry Edwin. They could all live in Portland happily ever after. Only her family hated the Morgans, and Edwin in particular. Edwin had a job in a mining company. He wasn't going to wait a year for her. In fact, if she didn't get a move on, he may leave without her tonight. No, nothing would come between her and her true love. Sarah walked purposefully toward the Orchard and into her dream life with Edwin.

CHAPTER 1

MINING VILLAGE–TYRELL'S PIT, NEAR BAKER CITY, MARCH 1861

Bear walked back to his camp, his heart heavy. Tyrell's Pit, while not a big town, was crawling with miners who would take great pleasure in killing one of his kind. Walking Tall had asked him to look for Miss Sassy as a favor. Walking Tall was worried about his friend Almanzo and the rest of his family following Rick's death. Miss Sassy had run away some time before her uncle had died. Did she even know he was dead? Did she care?

He had watched her for some time. It appeared she lived alone. She didn't seem to have any friends. There was no sign of the man she had run with. Bear wasn't surprised. He had followed that man, Morgan, for a few days. He was trouble. A drinker and a man who liked to play around with women. He had seen

Morgan with the saloon girls in the next town. He drank too much and had a vicious temper.

One night, Morgan had stumbled out of the saloon. He fell into some trash, disturbing a dog searching for food. The poor animal was skin and bones, but Morgan hadn't cared. He had kicked him repeatedly. The dog wasn't capable of defending himself effectively. Given the look of him, he was too weak from lack of food to match the strength of a man like Morgan.

Bear's hand squeezed around his knife as he remembered how Morgan had kicked that poor mongrel almost to death, only stopping when someone Morgan had known called him back to the saloon for more drink. Why did some men have to be so cruel?

Incensed anyone could be so heartless, Bear had been tempted to wait until Morgan came out again and beat him senseless. Instead, he had taken the animal back to his camp and, using all the medicines he knew, had helped the part-wolf, part-dog return to full health. How Tala, as he called him, had survived his injuries was beyond Bear, but then miracles did happen. For some.

He shook his head at the route his thoughts were taking. He had a duty to do. He owed Walking Tall a big debt, and this was his way of making repayment.

He would do his best to encourage Miss Sassy to go home. Now, before it was too late.

Bear lit a small fire to roast his dinner. Tala whined at him until he stroked the dog's fur. He was careful to keep the fire small, so there wasn't much smoke. Although he had checked many times, he didn't want to risk anyone seeing him there. Tala made a good watchdog; he would warn him if anyone got too close. Still, he wasn't going to invite trouble.

As he waited, he wondered why the family wanted the woman back. She was old enough to know her own mind. She had brought shame on her family. In his culture, maidens didn't run away like that. He knew in the white man's world, things were different. But from what he could work out, Miss Sassy had no reason to run away. She was well fed, lived in a nice home, and had a caring family. From what he had been told, Morgan hadn't kidnapped her. Miss Sassy had gone with the man of her own free will. She had chosen him as her mate. He was a horrible man and, yes, her family was right to be worried, but she was a grown woman.

It was completely different from the lifestyle he and his sister endured. He couldn't think of Snow Maiden now. The memory of his sister's death was still too painful. Walking Tall had been too late to save her and her child, but the magnificent warrior had ensured the evil man who had hurt his sister, among many others, lived no longer. He should have been the one to avenge his sister's honor, but he'd been too sick, his wounds having become infected due to lack of care. Walking Tall had taken him into his family and his women had cared for Bear so well, there were barely any scars left from his torture. The visible scars, that was. The internal scars were deep and festering.

He split the roasted meat between himself and Tala. Once their feast was over, he checked their camp area once more before bedding down beside the fire with Tala beside him. He kept licking Bear's face, as if the dog could tell his master wasn't in a happy mood. Once more, Bear wondered how any man could injure such a wonderful creature. The image of Edwin Morgan's face was the last he saw before falling into a deep sleep.

CHAPTER 2

TYRELL'S PIT, MINING VILLAGE, NEAR BAKER CITY, OREGON

Sarah Hughes looked up from the dirty water, wiping the sweat away from her forehead. Her hands were red and raw. There had to be a better way to make a living than washing strange men's underclothes. She looked toward the house at the far end of the town. The girls living there had lovely hands and nice clothes. She knew their work wasn't pleasant all the time, but surely it couldn't be worse than what she was doing. She wasn't an innocent anymore, so what could she lose by working there?

Your self-respect, or what's left of it. The little voice in her head seemed to scream at her. She closed her eyes, desperate to stop any tears from falling.

"Why have you stopped? That pile ain't going to get any smaller by sitting there."

"I know that," Sarah snapped back.

Mrs. Brown gave her a dirty look but didn't say anything else. She went back to the cafe she owned. Sarah knew the older woman thought she wasn't fit for the job. She'd told her often enough she'd only taken pity on her as Sarah reminded her of one of her own young'uns. The girl had looked a bit like Sarah, although younger. She'd been 17 when she succumbed to a fever outbreak that had decimated the entire town Mrs. Brown had once lived in.

Sarah plunged another shirt into the fresh water. Why did they have to wear the shirts until the collars were black before they handed them in to be laundered? She'd have to soak most of them or they would never come clean.

She turned to stir the whites she had boiling on the fire. The heat made her sweat even more. She could feel the damp spots under her arms and at the back of her neck. Her hair, although done up in a bun, was scraggly, hanging limply by the sides of her face. She must look horrific. But it didn't matter how she looked. Edwin had been gone for ages. He said he was never coming back. Did he mean it? Did she care? She touched her stomach. She wasn't totally alone, was she? He or she was part of the reason she was working so hard. When her condition became more evident, she wouldn't be able to stay. Mrs. Brown already thought she was a slacker. She would not employ an unwed mother.

"Slaving away I see, Mrs. Morgan?"

The skin on the back of Sarah's neck prickled as the man used the name she had taken to using when she'd found out she was pregnant. That was shortly after Edwin left, over a month ago. He was staring at her, undressing her with his eyes like he always did. She didn't have to look around to know. He'd done it even when Edwin lived in town.

"What can I do for you, Mr. Faulkner?" She was loath to address him, but she didn't have a choice. He was the most important man in town.

"Now there is an offer I didn't think I would receive," Faulkner said, his mean eyes trailing over her body in a blatant fashion. Sarah had the mad urge to pull the tub of hot water closer to her chest.

She decided to pretend she hadn't understood. "If you are here to collect your laundry, you must see Mrs. Brown. She prefers to handle the cash side of the business," Sarah said, trying to be polite. No fear of Mrs. Brown getting her hands wet.

"It's you I've come to see, as you well know. Have you given consideration to my offer? It's against the law of nature to allow a beautiful creature like yourself to work herself into the ground. Especially when the chores she is doing are best done by the Chinese women. It's all they are good for."

Sarah ignored his bigoted opinion. He sounded just like Edwin. How could she have ever believed she and Edwin had a future? His vile opinions had gotten worse as the days passed. His claim had dried up and somehow it was her fault. He had left her high and dry in the mountains, snuck out in the middle of the night, leaving a pile of debt. His biggest debtor was the man ogling her. Faulkner had made it clear exactly how she could pay off the bills Edwin owed.

"I didn't give your offer any more consideration than it was worth. My answer is the same as it was the first day you honored me with your proposal." Sarah adopted her coldest tone as she delivered her sarcastic answer. Jo would have been proud of her. Well, maybe not Jo. Her adoptive mother probably hated her and with good reason. She had behaved very badly, sneaking off to elope with Edwin. Why hadn't she listened?

If not to Rick and Jo, to Bridget. Their housekeeper had warned Sarah by speaking of her own experiences in a bad marriage. Well, at least Bridget's man had married her. Sarah was Mrs. Morgan in her own eyes only, not those of the law. Despite his promises, Edwin hadn't married her.

Faulkner's eye's narrowed. "Don't toy with me, girl.

There have been others, more mature in the ways of the world, who tried that. It didn't end well for them either."

"If you have had enough of threatening me, can you please leave? I have work to do and Mrs. Brown won't be happy if that pile doesn't get done." Sarah dismissed him as if he were nothing more than something unpleasant stuck to her shoe. His swift intake of breath gave her a quick jolt of pleasure before the stench of his breath on her cheek almost made her retch.

"I like spirit in my women. Not too much, mind you, but enough to make the getting to know one another rather interesting. You will give in to my demands, Missy. Better make it sooner than later if you know what's good for you." He took a step back, for which Sarah was grateful. Then, bowing deeply, he said mockingly, "Enjoy the rest of your day, my dear, don't work too hard."

She slouched against the wall at her back. What had she done that for? Faulkner was dangerous enough without her baiting him like that. She was too pigheaded and stubborn for her own good. And selfish. Mustn't forget that. If she hadn't behaved like a selfish, immature brat, she wouldn't be in her present predicament.

Sarah scrubbed the clothes, taking her anger at

Edwin, Faulkner, and the rest of the world out on her work. Mrs. Brown came to check on her later, but retreated at the look on Sarah's face. She had nothing to complain about—the pile of clean laundry being much higher than it had been.

Sarah had to do something, but what? She couldn't go home. Her parents may accept her after she groveled, but they would never take her back as an unmarried mother. She would have to have the baby and then have it adopted or something. Only then would she be free to return to Portland, Oregon, a single woman with no commitments or ties.

CHAPTER 3

Bear hid in the shadows, watching the white woman. His knuckles turned white holding the knife in his hand as the man tormented her. He didn't know what the history was between them, but this man meant to do her harm. Bear knew him. He had seen him before. Many times. He was a powerful man among his people.

He wanted to tell Miss Sassy she was safe, that he would protect her. But he couldn't do that. To come out of the shadows would be suicide. There were many in this camp who would take pleasure in killing one of his kind. As he watched, he smiled at her reaction. He could tell from her body language she was fighting back. She may be a woman, but she had the heart of a lion.

He shrunk back in the shadows as the man

stormed off. Whatever Miss Sassy had said, the man was angry and dangerous. His eyes narrowed as he spotted the glint of tears in her eyes. She would need closer watching. He wished he could just pick her up and take her home, but life wasn't that easy. For one thing, from what he had been told, she would fight him every step of the way. He must move slowly.

He waited until the older woman had left and it was time for Miss Sassy to go home. He moved quietly, too quietly, making her jump in fright when he reached her.

"Please do not scream. My name is Bear, and I come in peace."

"What do you want?" Sarah asked, hugging the wall of the store behind her, no doubt wishing she were on the other side.

"I watched you work hard all day with no food. I brought you this." Bear handed her a parcel. "You must stay strong and healthy."

"Thank you, but…I don't know you. Why would you help me?"

"I do not like the man who treats you bad. But I must go for now. I will come back."

And he was gone.

* * *

Sarah's heart had only just started beating normally again, and then he was gone. Who was he? Why was he really here? She looked around where he had vanished. Only his scent lingered, making her think of Walking Tall and the other Indians she'd known as a child. Those thoughts led to Almanzo, the boy who had been like a brother to her. He probably hated her, though, for running out on the family. He had been no fan of Edwin, either.

She clutched the package to her side as she walked back to her lodgings at Mulligan's store. It wasn't as big as the Newland's store back home in Portland, and the Mulligans were nowhere near as nice as the Newlands. Mr. Mulligan considered himself a religious man. But his version of religion was alien to Sarah. It involved a God who seemed to hate everyone and everything. He insisted his wife wear what he considered to be modest clothes. This included having her head covered at all times. Sarah smiled at the thought that homely Mrs. Mulligan was going to set any man's blood racing, but then wiped the smile from her face. Who was she to judge anyone? She wasn't one of their religious group, yet they had offered her shelter. She should count her blessings.

Opening the door to the side of the main storefront, she went inside quickly, locking the door behind her. Here she felt safe. Her home. A small room at the back of the store. The owners let her stay for a very low rent. They lived upstairs, but they wanted someone to sleep downstairs to discourage looters.

She sat at her small table and opened up her package. With wonder, she smelled the nuts and fruit the Indian had given her. Immediately, her mind was full of memories of the trail. Her family had traveled to Oregon by wagon train. Her ma and brothers had died from illness, so it was left to Uncle Rick and some of the other wagon train members to look after her and Carrie, her sister. Jo was one of the women who helped. She had fallen in love with Uncle Rick and the two married and had practically adopted the girls.

While on the trail, the Indians had often given them food to eat in exchange for Jo's help with medical things. Scott, their wagon train master, had grown up with the Indians so they were friendly to him and his charges. Sarah closed her eyes, inhaling the different scents of the feast in front of her. She pictured the Indian man. He was much taller than her and had wonderful black eyes filled with kindness. Tears fell freely down her face as she ate his gift. He'd been the first person to show her real kindness in a long time, and she didn't even know where he was from. Only his name. Later, as she lay in her bed, waiting for sleep, she wondered if she would see him again. It would be nice to have a friend.

CHAPTER 4

PORTLAND, OREGON

Tilly pulled up outside Newland's store. She had been practicing her baking and wanted Mrs. Newland to be her first victim. She didn't trust Almanzo's reaction. If she served her husband fried boots, he was bound to say they were delicious.

"Good morning, Tilly. You're in town early."

"I thought you might like some cookies with your morning coffee," Tilly said, smiling at the older woman. Her smile widened as she saw the look of horror cross Mrs. Newland's face before it was replaced with acceptance. "I promise I have improved lots. Though, I am not quite at Bridget's standard yet." Bridget had been coaching her when she had time, but Tilly thought it would be years before she would be as good at cooking as Jo's Irish housekeeper.

"Nobody can bake cookies like Bridget, dear. Jo and Rick were lucky when she came to live with them. Come inside and let me put the coffee on. I'm dying to hear all your news."

Tilly walked into the store, saying a quick hello to Mr. Newland before following his wife up the stairs into their private quarters. Fiona still lived there, but she was already at work helping the doctor at his office. Her experiences at the orphanage meant she had experience and patience with children, which was something Dr. White was extremely grateful for.

"It sure is quiet around here since you moved out, Tilly," Mrs. Newland commented as she set the table with cups and plates. Tilly put the basket down. Taking off her shawl, she hung it on the peg at the back of the door.

"I hope that isn't your way of telling me I was noisy, Mrs. Newland?" She loved teasing the older woman and watching her face turn pink. Mrs. Newland was one of the kindest women Tilly knew and she was proud to call her a friend.

"So tell me, how is Jo doing? We never see her in town, but I suppose that is because of the pregnancy. Has she heard anything from Sarah?"

Tilly's smile dropped at the mention of Jo's adopted daughter. Rick's own niece and she probably didn't know her uncle was dead. Almanzo said Jo and

Rick had treated Sarah like a daughter since her ma had died on the Oregon Trail. "No, nothing from Sarah. We have no idea whether she knows about Rick or not. Carrie wrote to her, but she hasn't even answered her sister. Carrie says she won't have anything to do with her but I suspect if Sarah did turn up, Carrie would welcome her with open arms." Tilly had seen Carrie's red-rimmed eyes even as she denied missing her big sister.

"Almanzo too, although he is likely to give her a stern talking to. They were very close on the trail up here. I thought sometimes they were going to end up married." Mrs. Newland stopped and blushed. "Sorry Tilly, I didn't mean any offense."

"None taken Mrs. Newland. I know she and Almanzo were close, but I think she always thought of him as a brother. He doesn't say much about her, although I know he was hurt when she ran off."

"And Jo? How is she?" Mrs. Newland asked, changing the subject.

"She's not doing too well. I mean, the pregnancy isn't making her ill, but she just seems so sad all the time." Tilly frowned, thinking of the woman who was like a mother to her. Almanzo's adopted mother for all intents and purposes. "Della is very worried about her. It's like she is an empty shell. She's there, but not there. If that makes sense. She looks after the twins and

Carrie, but she never smiles or laughs. She said the light of her life went out when Rick died."

"Poor Jo. I was ever so fond of Rick. He was a lovely man, always had time to help a friend or neighbor. He was a great teacher, too. Strict but fair. That new man can't seem to keep the children under control. The number of complaints we hear from the parents. If I charged them a dollar for every moan, I could retire a rich lady."

"Retire? You? Never. Portland wouldn't be the same without Newlands," Tilly said.

"You're too kind, dear. So tell me, what can I do to help Jo?"

"I don't know Mrs. Newland. I don't know anyone who lost someone they loved as much as Jo loved Rick."

"What does Almanzo say?" asked Mrs. Newland as she poured the boiling water into the coffee.

"You know what men are like. He thinks she'll get over it in time. Not that he doesn't miss Rick, of course he does. But he says with time, the pain becomes more bearable."

"Perhaps, but only when one deals with that pain. I will speak to the Reverend. He may be able to help." Mrs. Newland placed a steaming cup of coffee in front of them both and then sat down. She reached for a cookie, the look on her face like someone facing the gallows.

"They're nice this time. I promise. They won't break your teeth."

Mrs. Newland smiled, although whether at the joke or with relief, Tilly wasn't sure. She couldn't blame the woman. The last time she baked cookies, they had been so hard you could dent a wall if you threw one at it.

Mrs. Newland took a hesitant bite before beaming. "Tilly, these are good. In fact, I will have to save some for Mr. Newland. He loves dunking a cookie in his coffee, although he swears he doesn't do that."

Tilly smiled at the praise. At least she had gotten to grips with one task. The sheer volume of work involved with being a homesteader had surprised her. She was a hard worker, but everything was so new to her.

"You look tired, dear. Are you working too hard?"

"Oh Mrs. Newland, it never stops, does it? By the time I have all the chores done, I have to start over again. Why can't a house stay clean? It's not like we have a dozen children running around making it messy. There's only Almanzo and me."

"Don't be too hard on yourself Tilly. You had to learn from scratch. Most women who farm out here were born to it. You, well, you were born into a different kind of life altogether."

"I know, but we've been married almost eight months and I still burn the bread or singe his shirts. He must be sick of me."

"Dear now, don't be getting yourself into a state. He's not sick of you. Anyone with eyes in their head knows your husband adores you. Quite right, too. You're a lovely young woman with a heart of gold. You must stop being so hard on yourself. And you should learn to accept help when it's offered." Mrs. Newland stopped to take a drink. "Bridget was only saying the other day how much better you were managing."

"I don't know how I will get on if he has to go away," Tilly's sentence stopped mid-sob. Mortified at giving into her emotions, she stumbled through an apology but the words wouldn't come. Instead, her tears flowed.

"There now darling, let them fall. You aren't the first to shed tears over the situation our beloved country has gotten itself into and you won't be the last. We can only pray it doesn't come to war. If it does, we will pray the men get their heads straight, and it ends as soon as it starts."

"I'm sorry Mrs. Newland. I shouldn't have come here dragging my sorrows to you."

"You absolutely should. Who else are you going to

talk to? Poor Jo has enough to deal with. She doesn't want to think about Almanzo or her brother Stephen going off to fight. Della can't bear to speak of it. The Thompsons were always a close family, and Rick's death brought them even closer. You need to speak to someone who is outside that circle."

"Do you really believe there will be a war? Can't they do something to stop it?"

Mrs. Newland looked at her sadly. "I guess they could if they really wanted to, but I figure the mess has become too big for one man to solve."

Tilly decided it was time to change the subject. "Are you and Mr. Newland coming to our house on Sunday after church? All the family will be there, Blacky and Fiona, too."

"Are you sure we wouldn't be intruding?"

"Don't be silly. We want you with us. Just don't bring Mrs. Morgan with you."

Mrs. Newland gave Tilly a look. "The day I take that woman anywhere, the pigs will fly by your window."

Tilly jumped up and kissed Mrs. Newland on the cheek. "I've got to get back and start getting ready."

"But it's only Tuesday."

"Yes, but there is so much to do. I have to cook and clean and make sure...."

Mrs. Newland burst out laughing.

"What's so funny?"

"Tilly, you don't have to do everything yourself. Everyone will bring a dish with them. Now, off you go and let me get back downstairs to the store or Mr. Newland will be moaning again."

Tilly smiled gratefully at the older woman. She was lucky to have such lovely friends.

CHAPTER 5

TYRELL'S PIT.

The next few days passed and there was no sign of the Indian. Sarah had tried not to get her hopes up, but she was disappointed all the same. It would be nice to see a friendly face once in a while. She caught herself thinking of Walking Tall, Almanzo, Jo and Rick. And Carrie. Would her sister ever forgive her?

She sloshed the water around. Thankfully Faulkner hadn't come back to see her either, for which she was grateful. She was so engrossed in thinking about her own problems, she didn't see the child until he stood right next to her. She recognized him as belonging to one of the many families living in the shantytown nearer the mines.

"Mrs. Morgan, there's bad sickness at the mine. Can you come?"

Sarah looked at the barefoot child wearing rags. "Who are you? Why did you call me? What about the doctor?"

"He won't come. Said he wasn't paid the last time he went to the mine. I don't know if that's true, but my ma, she needs help. She said you helped her before. Her name is Joan Fallon. Mine is Johnny. Please come."

Sarah frowned. She couldn't remember his ma, but she had given a few pence to a mother whose baby was sick a couple of weeks back. She'd felt sorry for the thin, wretched looking creature. But giving a few pennies was different from visiting sick people. She didn't want to catch anything. "I'm sorry, Johnny, but I can't. I have too much to do here. Mrs. Brown would have my hide. I need this job more than anything."

Johnny stared at her, tears filling his eyes. "Ma will die. Please, won't you help us?"

Sarah turned her back on the boy and plunged more clothes into the hot, steamy water. She couldn't help. What did she know about nursing fevers? She wasn't a doctor or a nurse. No, the boy would have to find someone else. But who? There weren't that many women in town. She bit her lip. Could she let someone die? But she had the baby to think of. She looked back, but Johnny was gone. She pushed the clothes down furiously, kneading out the dirt. Using the arm of her dress to wipe the sweat from her forehead, she stared into the water, but in her mind, she saw Jo. Her Ma wouldn't have said no. Jo had helped save her life and the lives of their friends when they came by wagon to Oregon. Sarah had been told the story of how Jo had defied her father and gone to help an Indian woman who was sick. That had been Walking Tall's mother, who later died in a massacre. Jo wouldn't have thought twice about helping the boy.

* * *

Sarah washed more clothes, wondering whether the boy had gotten help or not. The hours passed slowly, despite her working harder than she ever had. Every time she took a rest, the guilt threatened to overwhelm her. Being pregnant was no excuse not to help the boy and his family. She was going to have the baby adopted as soon as it was born. She argued back and forth with herself all day. When Mrs. Brown arrived back, the look of surprise on her face when she saw how much laundry had been cleared, would have made Sarah laugh if she hadn't felt so guilty over the boy.

"Sarah, I asked you to work harder, not drive yourself into an early grave. You must have worked all day." Mrs. Brown looked at Sarah closely. "I ain't going to ask what's bothering you. Go home, lass, and get some sleep. Your shoulders and back will be aching tomorrow."

Shocked, her gruff employer actually seemed to care, if only a little, Sarah thanked her. Picking up her shawl, she wrapped it around her shoulders and stepped outside. There was a bite in the wind and, now she had stopped working so hard, the sweat on her skin was drying out. It would give her a chill if she didn't get home fast. Home. It sounded so much grander than it was.

Sarah reached the store without meeting anyone she recognized. She opened the locked door and walked through the store, savoring the different scents. Her stomach rumbled, reminding her she hadn't stopped for lunch. Again. Reaching her small room, she closed the door behind her and fell on the bed. Although hungry, she didn't have the energy to cook. She would make do with an apple and get up early to make flapjacks. Then she remembered the parcel the Indian had given her. She ate the leftovers with relish before she stripped, letting her clothes fall in a heap on the floor before diving under the covers. Shutting her eyes, she waited for sleep, but as soon as her head hit the pillow, she was wide awake.

If she closed her eyes, she kept seeing his face. The boy reminded her of Jake, Jo's six-year-old nephew. Only Jake looked healthy and well fed, had both his parents, Becky and Scott to look after him, whereas the boy from earlier was skin and bone, not to mention alone. She wondered where his pa was. Sick like his ma or down the mine? Maybe he had died in one of the many pit cave-ins. She had known Edwin's work could be dangerous, but until she came to live here, she had no idea of how often the men got buried under ground. Often they were never able to recover the bodies.

She tossed and turned, but it was no use. She knew she should have helped the boy and now she was paying for it. Getting up, she cooked a quick breakfast over the stove, thankful to her landlord that he had kept it lit overnight. It was another perk of staying at the store.

She was expected to do some chores to help toward the cost, like taking the family's laundry with her to work and returning it clean and neatly ironed. Sometimes she swept the store floor and occasionally she helped with the stock inventory, but that was the extent of it. Mr. and Mrs. Mulligan were good people. Mrs. Mulligan, especially, thought Sarah worked too hard. She had guessed Edwin had run off, but she didn't ask for details.

Was Edwin really gone for good?

CHAPTER 6

She ate one of the flapjacks and put the rest in a basket, along with some fruit and some bread Mrs. Mulligan had put aside for her the day before. She dressed in her warmest cloak and, turning the door handle, stepped out into the wee early morning. How would she find Johnny? She hadn't really given it much thought other than knowing the general location he had mentioned. With her shoulders back and taking a deep breath, Sarah walked quickly. She would check the boy's ma was okay and then she would return in time to go to work.

She made her way toward the shanty town. Despite the early hour, people were up. Women were cooking on open fires and children were running here and there. She kept looking for the boy but couldn't see him. Now she was here, she felt stupid. How would she find the mother if she couldn't find the son? She was about to turn back when she spotted him. She moved faster, closing the distance between them.

"Johnny, how is your ma?"

"What do you care? You wouldn't help yesterday." The boy didn't even look up at her. He stared sullenly at the ground.

"I'm here now, aren't I?"

Her sharp tone made him look up. Sarah took a step back at the anger in his eyes.

"Too late, she's dead. My brother too, my sister may as well be dead. Pa died in the last cave in. Only me now."

"I'm sorry," she whispered. "I'm so sorry."

"Don't pretend you care. You only think of yourself. Go back to your precious job."

"Johnny, you don't understand. I have to work. Here, I brought you some food."

"I don't want anything from you. Go away." The boy's scream made people turn around to stare at her. They didn't come to his aid, though. They were simply curious as to what was going on.

Sarah dropped the basket and turned back toward the town. The whole way back, the look in the boy's eyes occupied her thoughts. He hated her. She deserved it.

She arrived before Mrs. Brown, who didn't

comment when she saw the fires lit and the water boiling. Sarah worked as hard as she had the day before, but she couldn't shake her self-hatred. She scrubbed and scrubbed until Mrs. Brown told her to go home. "No point in making yourself ill. I don't know what's got into you, but this is taking things too far. You keep this up and you'll end up in the graveyard. You hear?"

"Mrs. Brown, have you heard anything about an outbreak of illness in miners' camp?"

"There is always illness up there. Comes from the foreigners. Don't know what they eat or why they never attempt to keep clean. Keep away from them, Sarah, if you know what's good for you. Nothing but trouble in that direction."

Sarah didn't argue. Mrs. Brown clearly didn't believe in helping her neighbors, so why did it bother Sarah so much? His look of hatred and sadness pierced her soul. She could hear him telling her she was selfish. He was right.

Just as she thought her day couldn't get any worse, when she went home, Mrs. Mulligan was waiting for her. It was obvious the landlady was upset, the anger coming at Sarah in waves. She racked her brain, wondering what she could have done to incur such wrath.

"Did you see him?"

Sarah stared at her landlady. See who? The Indian? Had he come back? Was this why Mrs. Mulligan was annoyed? She didn't get a chance to answer as the woman kept talking.

"I like you Sarah. In fact, I've become right fond of you. But I can't stand drunks."

Sarah looked at Mrs. Mulligan, wondering if her landlady had been drinking herself. Sarah never touched alcohol.

Then it dawned on her. Edwin drank. Could he be back? Sarah hated herself for the feeling of hope that rose in her chest. Once he knew about the baby, he would marry her. She wouldn't bring shame to her family. Babies came early all the time. Three months early! Sarah shook her head to clear her thoughts. Mrs. Mulligan's expression softened. Slightly.

"You didn't know he was back?"

"No Ma'am. Where is he?"

"Back in the saloon, I guess. I told him where you were working."

Sarah could feel the hope dying away, but she grasped it with both hands. He had returned, so he must feel something.

"Mrs. Mulligan, I am really sorry if he said or did anything to upset you. But can he stay here with me tonight? Tomorrow we will look for something more permanent."

The sour expression on Mrs. Mulligan's face disappeared. "Look, love, it's none of my business, but how did you get mixed up with a man like that? You're a nice girl with lovely manners. You didn't need to settle for that bowser."

But I love him. Or did she? Had she ever loved him? Regardless of that, it was too late now. Her baby needed a father, and she needed a husband. But she didn't say anything. Mrs. Mulligan believed her to be married.

"I know once you're married, you should try your best to make things work. Divorce is against the rules of God, but that man isn't right for you. He won't ever be kind or thoughtful and sure as my name's Mulligan, he will run off again."

Sarah shook her head sadly, despite knowing the woman spoke the truth. She didn't want to tell Mrs. Mulligan about the baby, as there was a risk Edwin would announce they weren't married. She had to speak to him.

"Thank you, Mrs. Mulligan. I will talk to Edwin and try to get him to curb his drinking and his behavior."

Mrs. Mulligan rubbed Sarah's arm. "You look after yourself, Sarah. I put this by for you earlier. You could make a stew, it would help to sober him up."

Sarah could have hugged her landlady. She had

nothing to make a meal with and Edwin wouldn't understand she hadn't expected him home. "Thank you."

"Mr. Mulligan says that God only sends us troubles we can deal with. It is to show us he loves us."

At this moment, Sarah didn't want love, which showered her in troubles. But she wasn't about to argue that point with Mrs. Mulligan.

She took the meat and quickly cut it into the smallest pieces so they would cook quicker. She put it on the stove with some onions and other vegetables. Then she cleaned her little space, trying to make it more homely looking. Finally, she set the table for two and waited. And waited.

CHAPTER 7

After some hours passed, she couldn't stay in her home any longer. She had to find him before he got too intoxicated. She didn't have anywhere else to go and couldn't risk the Mulligans throwing her out. She pulled a shawl over her head and shoulders and walked up to the saloon Edwin frequented most regularly when he lived in town.

Sarah walked up and down outside the saloon. She couldn't go inside, but she didn't want to miss Edwin, either. Finally, she got the courage to ask a man to ask Edwin to come out and speak to her. The man told her to go home and wait for her husband, but that was one luxury Sarah couldn't afford. She waited and waited until finally Edwin came out. He was furious, taking her arm, his grip so tight it hurt.

"How dare you show me up in front of my

friends? They are all talking about me being under the thumb of my wife. Funny that, as I don't have one. Do I?"

Sarah put her head down. She couldn't have this conversation in the middle of the street where anyone could hear. She tried using flattery to get him on her side.

"Edwin, darling, I heard you were home, and I was so excited to see you. I just couldn't wait. I'm sorry, but I cooked you a lovely meal. Wait and see."

He didn't look impressed, but at least he didn't call her anymore names. Instead, he walked down the street in the direction of the store. She brought him into her room, watching his eyes open at the meal she'd prepared. She had made a stew, as given Edwin's history, there was no telling when he would return and she didn't need anything to spoil on her tonight. The extra time on the heat would mean the meat was tender just how he liked. She served him and watched him eat. She couldn't chew a morsel as her stomach turned over and over.

"This is good. Your skills have improved. Who's been teaching ya?"

"Mrs. Mulligan, she owns the store."

"Pass on my regards, or maybe I will thank her myself. Is she young and pretty?"

Sarah bit her lip and counted to ten. She wasn't

going to let him wind her up. She had to remain calm. "I missed you Edwin."

"Don't start nagging me, woman. I went away to earn some money, heard of a gold strike in the next valley. But it was all gone when I got there. Good for nothing immigrants. They take everything."

Sarah refused to argue with him. She knew he was talking nonsense; the immigrants were some of the hardest working people she knew, but she needed to keep him in good form. "There are some jobs going in town. Safer ones. You could stay here and we could be together again."

He didn't respond.

"Edwin, I have something to tell you. You're going to be a Pa."

Sarah clenched her hands, willing him to be happy. But his expression was one of disgust.

"You couldn't wait to get me home to plant some other man's leavings on me. That isn't going to work, Sarah dear. Sure, it was fun but you and me, we haven't got a future. Ma told me you were no good. She was right. Didn't take long for you to give me what I wanted. No decent woman would do that."

"But that's not fair. I didn't have much choice in the—"

Bam. Her cheek lit up as his fist connected with it. Before she could react, he hit her another blow, this one sending her to the floor. She curled up in a fetal position, her instinct being to protect her baby. He aimed a few kicks at her before he left. She should have stayed where she was, but she didn't. He couldn't leave. Not now.

She picked herself up gingerly and ran out the door after him. "Edwin, wait, please. What about the baby?"

"Leave me alone woman, I need a drink."

* * *

BEAR STOOD IN A CONCEALED SPOT, having followed Edwin Morgan into town. He had only spotted the man, thanks to Tala's reaction. The dog's growls showed he hadn't forgiven the man who had almost killed him. Bear had left Tala back at camp for fear he would give his hiding place away. He had a bad feeling about Morgan being back in town. He hoped the man would not hurt Miss Sassy. She was suffering enough. He caught himself. Since when did he care what happened to a white woman? *Because*

Walking Tall instructed you to look out for her, he reminded himself. But he had only been asked to find her, see how she was faring, and then report back. Nobody said he had to stay in the area, making sure she was all right.

He stood near the saloon, waiting for Morgan to

reappear. Then he saw her. He wanted to tell her to go home. A woman never went into a saloon. What was she thinking? But he couldn't say or do anything. He watched her pace up and down before speaking briefly to a man. Soon afterward, Morgan came stumbling out. Bear's knuckles whitened as he watched Morgan grab her arm. He was tempted to intervene, but he couldn't. She wanted this man. At least her actions suggested she did. He faded back into the shadows and followed them back to the Mulligans' store. He would see she was safely home before he made his way back to camp. Tomorrow he would return to the Indians and tell Walking Tall what he had found out.

CHAPTER 8

Despite his words, Sarah ran after Edwin. She couldn't lose him now. But she also couldn't match his stride between her skirts and the pain in her side from where he'd kicked her. She soon fell to the ground.

And then someone was at her side almost immediately. He picked her up, whispering to her. She didn't understand everything he said, but enough to know she was to lie still. He carried her outside the town, through the forest to a small cave. The wind whistled through the branches behind them, but she didn't hear anyone following them. She wrinkled her nose as the scent of decay hit her. She sincerely hoped they weren't about to share the dwelling with any wild animals, especially not snakes. She wanted to ask him, but the blackness kept descending every time she lifted her head, so eventually she gave up. She heard a dog growling and whining. Dead leaves or twigs crackled underfoot as he moved farther into the cave, leaving the light behind them. Dimly she was aware of him laying her on something soft. And smelly. She groaned.

"Where are you hurt?" he asked, his accent triggering some memory in her brain which she couldn't quite place.

"Here," she pointed at her stomach.

"A fist or his foot?"

She looked into his face. Even in the dim light, she recognized him. It was the same man who had given her food a few days ago. She was so ashamed. He must have been watching her to have been able to help her so quickly. So he would know who did this to her.

"His foot…" Sarah whispered, not wanting to admit Edwin had kicked her. He had slapped her a few times before, but nothing like this. But he would kill her if she wasn't at the store when he came back. If he came back.

She tried to get up, but the pain was too much.

"Lie still. I will get you something for the pain. You cannot move. I do not know if you are hurt inside. I will be back soon."

He was back quickly with some water for her to drink. It tasted funny, but she was thirsty.

"But what if someone comes…"

"I will be here. You are not alone. Sleep."

She gazed into his face, his eyes full of concern. He cared what happened to her. Someone did. She closed her eyes, her last thought being how sad it was someone she didn't know.

* * *

Bear watched as she slid into a heavy sleep, the pain, hurt, and confusion disappearing from her face. He was shaking not just from anger at the torture the Morgan man had inflicted on Miss Sassy, but the look on her face, in her eyes, reminded him so much of Snow Maiden, his sister. She'd looked that way too when they were living with that man. Bear had intervened a few times, putting himself between his sister and the abuse she endured, but more often than not, he made things worse for her. It was hard to admit that. It had taken a long time for him to lose the guilt he felt. Walking Tall had helped him believe his sister would have died long before she did, if he hadn't been nearby.

He wasn't about to let another woman die at the hands of an abusive man. It didn't matter that this woman appeared to have chosen Morgan as her mate. Nobody deserved to be treated so badly. He sat watching her, wondering how much damage the man had inflicted. He wished Walking Tall, and the tribe were nearby. The medicine man may be able to cure her properly. His herbal remedies would soothe her pain and help her sleep. But it would not stop any injury from bleeding.

Through the night, he kept a close watch on her. Tala, without any prompting from him, lay across her feet, protecting her just as he protected Bear. The dog whined a couple of times as if asking why anyone would hurt someone else. But what could Bear say? There were men like Morgan in the Indian community too, but usually the elders kept them in check. Their wives were able to divorce these men and marry again. Although in the few cases Bear had been witness to, the women chose to remain single.

Couldn't Miss Sassy just leave this man, too? Was she really married to him? She called herself Mrs. Morgan. At least that is how the boy had greeted her when he'd asked her for help. Bear stared at the woman lying on her side. He'd been shocked when she'd refused to help the child. She had reconsidered, and he had followed her to the camp the next morning, but it had been too late by then. Snow Maiden would have helped any child who asked her. How could he think this woman reminded him of his beloved sister?

CHAPTER 9

Sarah woke early the next morning, the unusual smell of her surroundings reminding her where she was. Her side throbbed as much as her cheek, but she didn't feel faint anymore. Whatever the man had given her last night had helped her sleep and got rid of the pain. She wished he could give her more. But she couldn't afford to sleep. She had to get to work or she would lose her job.

She stood, grimacing as her head hit an out-jutting piece of rock. That was all she needed. The Indian must have heard her moan as he was beside her in an instant.

"You should not move. You need rest."

"Thank you, but I have to go. I must work," Sarah protested, even as she rubbed her head.

"No! You need rest, not work. You are hurt."

"I need my job. If I don't work, I can't eat." She knew she was being stubborn, but her job was the only thing standing between her and utter ruin. "Thank you for your help. You were very kind."

He shrugged.

"I don't know how to repay you." For a second Sarah thought of how Edwin and men like him would expect to be paid, but instead of demanding anything, the Indian surprised her.

"You said thank you. If you are sure you will go back to town, I will help you. We cannot risk being seen. We must go now when it is still early."

Sarah nodded, having lost the ability to talk due to the pain. But she couldn't let him know it was this bad. He led her silently out of the cave, the light outside making her blink. It had rained overnight, leaving the forest glistening with water droplets. She was thankful it wasn't raining now. Mrs. Brown wouldn't take kindly to her arriving looking worse than she felt. She swayed slightly as a rush of pain hit her. He glanced at her.

"I'm fine. And I have to work. I need the money."

He obviously didn't believe she was fine. He lifted her into his arms and ran with her to the edge of town. Then he set her gently on her feet. "You must be careful."

"Thank you," Sarah smiled at him. "I am very grateful."

The Indian smiled. "You are welcome." And then he was gone. Sarah limped back to the store, wondering if Edwin was waiting for her. How would she explain her absence? But he wasn't there. Torn between relief and concern that he hadn't come home, she washed herself quickly and headed to work.

The laundry owner's intake of breath reminded Sarah she hadn't looked in the mirror.

"He'd been drinking, I see. Can't understand how some treat their wives so badly. You best go see the doc."

"I can't afford to. I'll be fine." Sarah hoped that if she said she was fine often enough, it would come true.

Mrs. Brown shrugged her shoulders. "Your decision I guess. She eyed Sarah for a minute and then walked away muttering, "Those shirts won't clean themselves."

Sarah pushed her hair out of her eyes and, taking as deep a breath as possible, she began to work. It was pure agony, but she had to keep going. She wondered where Edwin had gone now. Was he ever going to marry her? Did she really want to tie herself to a man like that? Bit late now. As Grandma Della would say, she had made her bed and now she had to lie in it. She wiped the sweat from her forehead, wincing at the movement. She would give anything to be home in Portland, but her family wouldn't accept her. Not now.

CHAPTER 10

She worked hard for most of the day, trying to ignore the stabbing pains in her stomach. Her cheek ached too, not to mention the lump on her head. Mrs. Brown let Sarah go home early, another unexpected kindness. As she trudged along the street, she hoped nobody she recognized would see her. All she wanted to do was fall into bed and try to seek refuge in sleep.

"About time you showed up. Is a man expected to cook his own dinner?"

Sarah opened and closed her mouth like a fish. He had a nerve. He hadn't even winced at the bruise on her face or noticed how slowly she walked. He really was a self-centered son of a...

She ignored him as she started to prepare a meal she didn't want. If she didn't feed him, he was likely to beat her again and her body couldn't stand much more. She heated up the previous night's leftover stew in silence, but he didn't comment. As soon as she put the plate in front of him, he started shoveling the food into his mouth and didn't speak again until the plate was clean. No word of thanks, either.

"Met Faulkner last night. He's agreed to let you work off our debt."

Sarah couldn't move. She didn't believe what she was hearing. Instinctively, she picked up the ladle she'd used to reheat the stew. She turned toward him, holding the ladle in the folds of her dress.

"What did you say?"

"You heard. Don't look at me like that. It's not like you don't enjoy it. Now you can earn some money at the same time."

"I won't do it," she forced every ounce of confidence into her voice.

"Yes, you will." He didn't even look at her.

"No, Edwin, I won't. I am not going to entertain any of Faulkner's friends, or yours for that matter. I am not that type of girl."

He was quicker than she realized and was right in her face, twisting her arm painfully behind her back.

"But you are, aren't you Sarah? Where were you last night? You didn't sleep in my bed and you weren't here, so whose bed did you warm?"

Sarah wanted to hit him with the ladle, but she couldn't reach. Not when he had her pinned against the wall, her other hand behind her back.

"I hate you," she hissed at him.

He laughed. "Do I look like I care? I'm only thankful I didn't marry you. I…"

"Move away gently, lad, or you will have a sore head."

Panic made his eyes flare as Mrs. Mulligan stood over him with a piece of wood in her hand. He moved toward her, but she was ready for him.

"Don't even try it. Mr. Mulligan, he's right outside and he don't take kindly to anyone manhandling me. Now leave Sarah alone and get out of here while you still can."

Edwin looked from the woman to the wooden weapon and back at her face. Obviously deciding she was a serious threat, he quickly released Sarah. "She's nothing but a whore, anyway. You are welcome to her and her brat!"

Sarah couldn't see Mrs. Mulligan's face through her tears. She was mortified, not only because her landlady had to rescue her, but now she knew both her secrets. She wasn't married, and she had a babe on the way. Edwin grabbed some of Sarah's belongings, but she was too distraught to argue. And then he was gone. Mrs. Mulligan made sure he had left before locking the door behind him. She came back into Sarah's room. Sarah hadn't moved from the wall. Her legs didn't feel too steady.

"He's a right nasty piece of work. What's a girl like you doing with a man like that?"

"I thought he loved me. He wanted to marry me, but now…"

"Aw lass, you made a mess of things, haven't you? I wish there was something I could do for you, but Mr. Mulligan, he won't stand for any carrying on. He has to think about his position as an elder in his church. If it were up to me, I would let you stay, but you will have to go after tonight."

Sarah couldn't believe what she was hearing. "You're throwing me out? But I have nowhere, no one." She hated begging, but she didn't have any choice.

"You should have thought about that before you engaged in…well you know. Goodnight dear. I hope things work out for you. I truly do."

Mrs. Mulligan left as Sarah stared at her in silence. There was no point in arguing. Mr. Mulligan had very strict opinions, and there was no way he would help her. In his eyes, she was exactly what Edwin had called her.

She sat at the table in despair. What was she going to do now?

CHAPTER 11

Bear sat at his makeshift camp. He had packed up earlier with the intention of going home, but something had stopped him. Or rather, someone.

He didn't want to admit that he was worried about Miss Sassy. Of course, he didn't trust Morgan, but she was old enough to make her own choices. Bear half considered kidnapping her and taking her forcefully back to Walking Tall and the others. But that wouldn't work. Walking Tall wouldn't thank him for bringing the Army on top of them. Miss Sassy would hate him, too. No, it was best he leave her to her life and try to get on with his own. What was he going to do when he returned to the main camp? He had no reason to stay. He had paid back his debt to Walking Tall. Well, as much as he could. How could you repay someone for saving your life?

And he couldn't stay among the Indians, not anymore. While they accepted him, the elders wouldn't let their daughters mate with him. Just like Tala, he would never fit in one world. Tala and his offspring would never be accepted as wolves or as dogs. He was a mongrel, just like Tala. His mixed blood would pass on to the next generation. Maybe he could go and join the army. War was coming. He knew that from the little he had heard from the whites. He could fight against those who held the black people in irons. But would the army accept him? Wasn't he just as red as his mother? In their eyes?

He closed his eyes. He hadn't thought about his mother in a long time, his memories of her having faded over the years. He remembered her washing her long jet black hair and drying it near the fire. His father, or the man he assumed was his father, had been in the army. He had loved his mother, of that Bear had no doubt. He had seen the way the man had looked at her and held her, but he didn't love her enough to acknowledge her in public or bring him back to live with him at the fort. His mother had drowned herself when she found out he was marrying a white woman.

She had let herself believe he would marry her and introduce her to the white man's world. Bear had been eight and Snow Maiden had been fourteen when they'd found her. Snow Maiden had looked after him for a while until John Redskin arrived. He was about ten years older than Snow Maiden and seemed kind. He was from a mixed relationship too, said he understood their lives and would look after them both. But he hadn't.

Walking Tall had taken him to his camp, into his teepee. His women had cleaned his cuts and saved him from infection. Then the braves had coached him in the art of self protection. He could kill silently now with his bare hands or his knife. He had all the skills he would have learned if his mother had returned to live with her tribe, which had cast her out years before. Walking Tall's family was like a family to him, but he knew he was ultimately on his own. Just him and Tala.

Bear shifted again. He would check on Miss Sassy one last time before he returned to Walking Tall's camp. He owed his friend that much, at least.

* * *

AFTER A FITFUL NIGHT'S SLEEP, Sarah gathered her meager possessions. What was she going to do? There were no suitable lodgings in the town that she could afford. She stifled a tear. No point in giving into tears as that wasn't going to do her any good. She cleaned the room, leaving it tidier than when she had moved in. Mrs. Mulligan was nowhere to be seen. Mr. Mulligan took the key without a word. If she had any doubts that Mrs. Mulligan had been wrong about her husband's views, they vanished immediately at the look on his face. He didn't even meet her eyes. To him, she was a soiled dove. Someone whose existence tainted his person.

Closing her eyes, she said a quick prayer for guidance. She couldn't help wishing she were back at home with Jo, Rick, Carrie, and the rest of her family.

CHAPTER 12

PORTLAND, OREGON

Jo looked out the window of her newly built home. It had a different shape than the one she had shared with Rick. The one that had burned down. Rick. She knew she'd miss him, but she hadn't been prepared for the painful reality. Every day she woke up thinking she must tell Rick something only to find the empty space beside her. She rubbed a hand over her swollen stomach. Their baby was due in a month. Jo closed her eyes. She had to be both father and mother to this child. She didn't have time to dwell on her loneliness or the fact she hadn't gotten to say goodbye. Rick would expect her to go on with her life and provide a happy childhood for Carrie, the twins, and this little one.

"Would you like a cup of tea, Miss Johanna?" Bridget asked, popping her face around the bedroom door. "I am right glad you took my advice and had a sleep in. You won't get much sleeping done when the little one is born."

Jo lowered her body into the chair near the window. She was tired, her ankles were swollen and her emotions were all over the place.

"You feeling all right, Miss Johanna? You look very pale."

"I had another dream. I didn't want to wake up," Jo said. "I miss him so much."

"I know, love, and you'll go on missing him. Mr. Rick, he was one of the nicest men I've known. He would be so proud of you, the way you have cared for this family. Carrie and the twins are lucky to have you as a mother."

"Bridget, you won't leave me, will you?"

"Never. Whatever gave you that idea?" Bridget looked shocked.

"I was reading in the paper about the women who are going to work as nurses or cooks for the army if there is war. I wondered if you would want to go."

"Not in a million years, Miss Johanna. War is never right. I don't care what the men say. The only people who benefit from wars are those that make gunpowder and cannons. The rest of us suffer. Nobody really wins and I don't think any problem is ever solved." Bridget stood, hands on her hips, as if she were about to do battle with someone. "Truth be told, if men had babies, they wouldn't be so quick to start wars. And they say women are the weaker sex. Hmph!"

Jo couldn't resist smiling. Once Bridget got annoyed, her Irish temper flared like a lit match. She hadn't realized how strongly the woman disagreed with the war.

"Now, Miss Johanna, that doesn't mean I won't do my bit. I will knit socks and scarves just like every other woman in America. But I will do it after I look after you and your family. You are my priority."

Tears filled Jo's eyes. "Thank you, Bridget, but it's our family. Everyone considers you part of it. We adopted you just as we adopted Carrie and Almanzo. I wish you could call me Jo. Miss Johanna is way too formal. Couldn't you try it? It would make me so happy."

"Oh now, Miss Johanna," Bridget paused at Jo's raised eyebrows, "Jo, you aren't being fair. You know I would do just about anything to try to make you happy. "

"Well, calling me by my name isn't a lot to ask, is it?" Jo said, a mischievous smile on her face. "While you are at it, Miss Carrie and Mr. Almanzo would prefer you called them by their first names too."

"Miss—I mean, Jo, you are wicked. You got me, so I

can't say no to you. I never did see a servant call her mistress by her first name."

"You are not, and never were, our servant. I will cook tonight to prove that to you."

"Jo, I might love you, but no thank you. I do the cooking in my kitchen. Now I'm going to get you some tea. You stay where you are and put your feet up on the stool. Doc White said you had to take things slower now."

"Anyone would think I was an old woman," Jo grumbled.

"No, they wouldn't. Old people are sensible." With that passing remark, Bridget disappeared. Jo smiled. She couldn't help it. Bridget's down-to-earth nature and her obvious love for the family always cheered her up.

She picked up one of the newspapers Carrie had brought her back from town and began to read, frowning as she did so. The article said Allan Pinkerton had to escort the President elect, Abraham Lincoln, to Washington because he was worried about a protest from some Southern leaning groups that were unhappy when the President was inaugurated on March 4th.

Jo closed her eyes, remembering one of her last conversations with Rick. He had explained to Fiona Murphy, Tilly's friend, how, while Lincoln was antislavery, he did not believe in equality. She wondered if the President had changed his mind. Some were hopeful he would, but Jo wasn't sure. What she was certain about, though, was the fact the country stood on the brink of war. She didn't know if Almanzo and Stephen would volunteer to go. There wasn't, as yet, talk of conscription, although her pa thought it would come. Maybe the boys would wait to go later. Almanzo was busy helping her, Stephen was helping his parents. Both were needed here.

"Here's your tea, Miss—I mean—Jo," Bridget's eyes twinkled. "It may take some time to get used to your new name. What are you reading about?"

"President Lincoln and how they were worried someone would kill him before he became president."

"There is so much hate in this country right now. It's disgusting. Why can't people just get along?"

"I don't know. I'm worried Stephen and Almanzo will be called up to fight. I can't bear to think of them going off to war."

"At least this far west, the war isn't likely to come to our front door. I sure wouldn't want to live in Richmond right now or in any place nearby. Imagine having a battle on your front lawn."

Jo shuddered before saying. "Let's talk about something nicer. What's happening in town? Have you heard anything interesting?"

"Tilly said Fiona and Blacky are closer than ever. Might even get married."

"That would be lovely, wouldn't it? Fiona is such a nice girl. And Blacky's a gentleman. They're a good match, although I don't envy her dealing with his sons. Rick always said they were a handful."

"I heard they were a bit wild. Can't imagine Blacky has much time to deal with them as he's so busy working. Did his wife die long ago?" Bridget asked.

"I have no idea. I never met her. In fact, I don't know anything about Blacky's personal life. But I do hope he and Fiona will be happy together."

Bridget laughed. "Look at us, we have them married already and I don't know if he's even asked her yet." Bridget walked out of the room but stopped to remind Jo about Tilly's gathering the next day. "We can ask Blacky what his intentions are, then."

Jo frowned as Bridget closed the door behind her. Why had she agreed to go to Tilly's party? *Because she is as close to you as a real daughter-in-law and needs your support.* Almanzo had asked Jo to help and she couldn't say no. But oh, how she wished Rick was by her side.

She closed her eyes and thought about Sarah, Rick's niece. They'd considered her and Carrie as their daughters. Where was Sarah now? Did she know about Rick? Much as she was angry at Sarah for running away, especially with a man like Edwin

Morgan, Jo wanted more than anything to know she was safe and happy. The world was becoming more dangerous by the minute. The talk of war had many people on tenterhooks, and Sarah was out there in the middle of it somewhere. She wanted her to come home where Jo could see for herself that Sarah was happy, safe and sound. Even if she came back with Morgan in tow, she would accept her adopted daughter's choice. *Just please come home*, she prayed.

CHAPTER 13

TYRELL'S PIT

Sarah walked slowly down the street toward the laundry. She was late for work, but that was probably the least of her problems. Faulkner stood near the laundry. She tried to hurry past him, but he blocked her way.

"Had an interesting chat with your *husband, Mrs. Morgan.*" His sneering voice and the look in his eyes made Sarah turn and walk down an alley between two properties. It was a mistake. He had her pinned against the wall of one house in seconds.

"Don't walk away from me, girl. You're in no position to look down on anyone."

"Let me go. If you don't, I'll scream."

He laughed. "Scream away. Nobody will hear you and even if they do, they aren't going to come to your rescue. Not when they see me. I own this town, Sarah, and everyone in it."

"You don't own me," Sarah protested, backing away from him.

"I think you're wrong. You have nobody else. You have a brat in your belly, your man has walked out on you. Worse, he sold you to me so you could work off his debts. That work starts today."

"He can't sell me. I'm not a slave."

"Who says he can't? I don't see any law around here."

Sarah couldn't think straight. She was too horrified, scared, and angry. How dare he treat her like a...a what? A slave? Was that how slaves felt? She had never thought about it before, being too wrapped up in her own life. She shuddered. The anger that had been building up since Edwin had first shown up grew stronger. Despite the pain in her side, she was not going to become a soiled dove without a fight. She let herself go limp in Faulkner's arms, leading him into a false sense of security.

"That's better. You're a sensible girl. You know when you're beaten." He leaned in closer, almost whispering to her now. "Don't become too placid. I like a bit of fight in a woman."

"Good!" Sarah screamed as she slapped his face as hard as she could. She couldn't kick him between the legs as her skirts restricted her aim, but once he put his hands up to his face, she lifted her skirts and ran. She almost got away, but he was too quick.

"You little bi—"

Sarah hit him again and again, fighting with every bit of strength she possessed, but it was pointless. He was bigger, stronger, and better fed. He let her fight, and then, when she was almost winded, he backhanded her. Falling to the ground, she seized a stone, intent on using it.

"Sarah, Sarah, why persist? You can't fight me."

"No, but I can. Keep away."

Sarah recognized the voice. She watched Faulkner closely as he turned, his face pale until he saw who had spoken. Then he laughed. "You? You can't touch me. You know the penalty for hurting a white man. I'd have you strung up from the nearest tree, you savage."

"You're the one beating a woman." Bear looked Faulkner up and down with obvious loathing. "Sarah, come. We leave. Now."

Faulkner stood between Bear and Sarah. "She's mine. She stays."

"She is a free woman. Nobody owns her. She can come if she wants to."

Sarah struggled to stand up, the pain in her side worse than ever. She had used almost all her energy fighting Faulkner, but this was her chance to escape.

She crawled a little until she could pick herself up. Bear took a step toward her, but Faulkner pulled his gun.

"I told you, she ain't going nowhere. You leave now, or I'll put a bullet in you."

Bear didn't move a muscle, but his eyes focused on the gun. "Sarah, go now. Wait for me. Where we met before."

"But he'll shoot—"

"Go. Now."

Sarah turned to go, but in that instant, she saw Faulkner raise his gun and she remembered the stone in her hand. With all the force she could gather, she hit Faulkner on the side of his head. He looked stunned for a moment before he fell over. His head hit a rock as he met the ground. Bear bent down quickly to check.

"He's dead, isn't he? I just killed a man. Oh my God, what am I going to do? I didn't mean to. I just wanted to escape."

"Shush, Miss Sassy, you will attract attention. We have to get out of here now."

"We can't just leave him here. Like that."

"We have to. Come now."

"But—"

"Miss Sassy, Sarah, we must go. If we don't, I am a dead man."

In her horror, it took Sarah a few seconds to realize Bear was right. The townsfolk wouldn't believe a girl her size would be able to kill Faulkner. They would blame the Indian; he wouldn't even get a trial. They would just lynch him. She looked at him, seeing double. She swayed and was about to fall when he caught her and ran.

She kept her eyes shut as they moved through the forest, hoping that would stop her from being sick. Bear didn't make much noise as he moved. She heard a couple of squirrels, their claws scrabbling against the tree bark. The air was scented with wild mint, as it had been the last time he had saved her. So she knew they were nearly at the cave again. Was it only two nights ago that she had her first visit? It seemed so much longer. Her life as she knew it was over. It hadn't been comfortable or good, but at least she'd known what to expect. Now she had to start over. Alone.

But was she? She had a baby to consider. She squeezed her eyes shut. Now wasn't the time to feel sorry for herself. They finally reached the cave without incident. Sarah stood while Bear went inside to make sure no wild animals had taken over the space.

Sarah couldn't help but empty her stomach. She heaved until there was nothing left and then heaved some more. Bear brought her water and then made her go inside to lie down and rest. She walked slowly, not wanting to hit her head again. The cave smelled damp, and she could hear water dropping onto the floor. Was that from the recent rain? Bear had lain the furs down on a dry area of the cave. In that section, Sarah found she could stand up without fear of hitting the sides of the cave. She relaxed slightly. For the moment, they were safe. Nobody seemed to have chased them. The cave was well hidden from the forest and, given Bear's care in taking her here, she assumed he had covered his tracks well enough.

She lay down, but still she didn't think she would ever sleep again. Every time she closed her eyes, she saw Faulkner's face, his eyes staring but seeing nothing. Shuddering, she dragged the blankets around her. Her body felt funny, and she began feeling very sleepy. Bear must have put something in the water. She should be scared of losing control, but it was such a relief. And she trusted Bear. She didn't know why, she just did.

* * *

ONLY ONCE SHE was in a deep sleep did Bear leave her. He left Tala to watch over her. He had no option but to check on whether they were being followed. He went as close to the town as he dared, but there was no sign of any unusual activity. Maybe the townsfolk hadn't yet discovered the body. Or perhaps they had and just assumed someone who had been a victim of Faulkner's killed him. Rich and powerful men like him tended not to be too popular, as invariably they made their money off the backs of the miners. Bear was torn between taking a closer look around the town and getting back to check on Sarah. He knew if she woke up alone she would be scared, so he decided to go to her. Despite not seeing any upset in the town, he didn't want to tempt fate. It was best for everyone if they put as much distance between themselves and this town.

CHAPTER 14

PORTLAND, OREGON

Sunday came around very quickly. Thankfully, it was quite a sunny day so the Hughes family could eat outside. Mrs. Newland had been right. Everyone brought a dish with them so the tables creaked under the weight of all the food. The only thing missing, as far as Tilly was concerned, were their Indian friends. But Walking Tall didn't think it was safe to come down from the mountains.

Family events weren't the same without Rick. Tilly took a deep breath and told herself that today was not the day for tears. She was the hostess, and it was her job to make everyone comfortable, not upset them.

Later that afternoon, when their bellies were fit to burst and the party members lounged around talking and enjoying each other's company, Tilly heard hoofbeats on the road to their house.

When the rider came into view, she saw it was a soldier. He looked so excited, she knew immediately that something was wrong. Please God, don't tell me they are going to attack Indians again.

"It's happened," he said. "We are at war."

The men crowded around the stranger to find out more details while the women gathered together, hoping their menfolk wouldn't be leaving them. Tilly was determined to carry on as if nothing were happening. If she didn't acknowledge the war, then she didn't have to worry about Almanzo joining up.

"Almanzo, what are you going to do?" David asked.

"I don't know. Part of me wants to fight for my country, but the other part wants to stay here and protect my family. One thing is for sure, I won't fight against the Indians."

"Why would you go into battle against Indians?" Tilly asked.

"The newspapers are reporting that the regiments formed in Oregon and California will be stationed here to keep the Indian 'situation' under control. Tensions are rising and it's only a matter of time before something happens. The Indians aren't going to go willingly to reservations. And who could blame them?"

"So if you join up in Oregon, you could end up fighting against Walking Tall and his friends." Tilly put her thoughts into words, even though she couldn't quite believe them.

"My friends too, Tilly." Almanzo smiled, though his eyes were sad. "I can't do that. I won't raise a gun against innocent people or fight for something against my beliefs. What do you think, David?"

Tilly looked at Jo's brother-in-law. He was a very knowledgeable reporter working for the Oregon Echo. Most of the family looked to him for advice now that Rick was gone. Scott, Jo's other brother-in-law, was very knowledgeable on the area and all things Indian related. Between the two of them, there was little they didn't know.

"I agree with you, Almanzo," David said. "If you join up, you become a soldier and must obey orders. If you are ordered to fight Indians and refuse, you could end up shot as a deserter or go to prison. Neither of which is a good option."

"So, do I stay out of it altogether?" Almanzo asked.

"I can't make that decision for you."

"And why not? You seem to make decisions for other people without having a problem with it," David's wife, Eva, said.

Uncomfortable at the atmosphere between the couple, Tilly gave Almanzo a look, but before they could leave David and Eva alone, David answered his wife.

"Eva, I know you disagree with me, but I have to go. It's my duty."

"Your duty is to your wife and family. You promised to protect me. What about our boys?" Eva said, her eyes glistening with un-spilled tears.

David moved to her side, taking her in his arms. Tilly wanted to close her eyes or have the ground open up and swallow her rather than witness this private moment between the couple.

"Eva, I love you and our children. You're part of the reason I have to go. Newspaper men have a duty to report the truth. I can't stand here and watch other people fight for what I believe in. I need to join up and fight for freedom for the slaves. But my editor says an honest newspaper man is of more value to the cause than another dead soldier."

At his words, Eva shuddered. Tilly didn't blame her. She dreaded the thought of anything happening to Almanzo. She grabbed his hand, holding it between the two of hers. Losing her father-in-law was horrible, but the grief would be nothing compared to losing the love of her life. Eva was probably thinking the same thing, having loved David ever since they were both children.

"Maybe I'm being selfish, but also I want to see what Lincoln achieves. He was almost the Governor of Oregon, only his wife, Mary, didn't want to live this far west. Our own Edward Baker introduced him at his inaugural."

"Why can't you write the stories for our newspaper here? Surely you don't need to leave to report on the war?" Eva asked.

Tilly had never seen this side of Eva before. Jo's elder sister was usually so composed and in control. She edged Almanzo, trying to hint they should walk away, but her husband seemed to be listening to David intently. A little too intently. Surely Almanzo wouldn't go too? She pulled at his arm.

"Excuse us, my wife is giving me a hint to leave you both alone," Almanzo said.

"Please excuse us, Tilly. We should have kept our discussion private. It's just we never seem to get time to talk these days, do we, David?" Eva apologized, blushing.

"It's quite alright," Tilly said. "Please don't worry. We're family, after all. Why don't you two go on home and we can keep the boys for the night? That will give you some time alone."

Eva gave her a quick hug. "Thank you, Tilly. You are an angel. Thank heavens Almanzo married you and not Sarah."

Tilly didn't have time to react to that remark as Eva and David almost ran from the party. They obviously relished the chance to spend some time alone.

Was that what it would be like for her and Almanzo if they ever had children?

"Almanzo, are you going to join up?" she asked him, hoping he wouldn't hear the fear in her voice.

"Darling, I don't know yet. Nobody knows what's going to happen. We have to wait and see."

"But you could be killed…" she said, hating the tears that made her voice shake.

"I promise if I have to go, I will do everything I can to come back safely. Even if I don't go to war, there are no guarantees I would be safer here. We only have to look at what happened to Rick to see that."

She wrapped her arms around his neck. "I don't want you to go, and I couldn't bear it if you died. But I know I'm being selfish."

"No, you aren't. David and Eva's talk upset you, that's all."

"Although if you did go, I wouldn't miss your socks." Tilly smiled, linking her arm through his and trying to recapture the good mood of earlier.

"What are you saying? My socks don't smell. If you keep complaining, I will send you up to the mountains and ask Walking Tall to cover you in bear grease," Almanzo said, laughing at the expression on her face.

"No thank you, but I do think it would be a good idea to go check on Mia. It's been months since she left. I wonder how she's doing? It's a lot for a young girl to lose her ma and granddad and all those friends."

Tilly knew children were often more resilient than adults, but Mia had lost her ma and granddad during an Indian massacre.

Almanzo kissed her forehead. "I love you more every day, Tilly. I will go and see Mia."

"Your ma was wonderful to me and Fiona when the Indians found us. It was her that made us see not all Indians were bad and that the tribe was trying to protect us."

"Some of them wanted to do more that protect you. You could have become a squaw, too."

Tilly gave him a playful swat on the arm. "I wanted to talk to you about something. You know I said before that I wanted to give Fiona some money so she could start her orphanage?"

"Yes, but I thought she turned you down."

"She did. But I was wondering if we could approach it in a different way. What about building a combined school and orphanage on our land? Then we can suggest Jo comes in as a teacher and Fiona looks after the orphans. It would help get Jo out of the house."

"But Jo's about to have a baby," Almanzo said, staring at his wife.

"I know that," she swatted his arm. "But when the

baby is a little bigger, she can bring him or her to the school with her. Fiona could look after the baby while Jo is working. Jo needs something to occupy her mind, and a baby isn't enough. She has to focus on something. She was telling me it was Rick's dream to provide an education to all children. So I thought we could call it the Hughes Orphanage or Rick's place or something to remember him by."

Almanzo grabbed Tilly and swung her around until she was dizzy. "That's a wonderful idea. I know just the spot, too. Down near the trees in the south pasture. It's a nice area, but the land is too rocky to be good for farming." His eyes blazed with excitement, filling Tilly with pride. She was so happy he approved of her idea. "But let's not tell anyone until we find out we can do it. I'm sure some of the townsfolk will help. Blacky is a popular man and they seem to have accepted you and Fiona a bit more as well." Almanzo kissed her again. Then he spotted Stephen just a little way up the road. Almanzo gave her a quick peck on the cheek before he left to speak to Stephen.

Once he'd left, the smile drained from her face. Not everyone accepted her. Some of the townsfolk still believed she and Fiona Murphy should have committed suicide after living with the Indians, even though they hadn't been defiled in any way. Only last week, Mrs. Morgan had called her a horrible name, but she hadn't told Almanzo. It was pointless upsetting him when he was already worried about Jo and the baby, never mind Sarah. Nobody had heard from her in months. Jo had been devastated when Sarah didn't respond to her letter telling her about Rick's death. Almanzo hadn't said much about it, but Tilly knew he had been hurt, too. Carrie had written to Sarah, telling her not to bother ever coming back to Portland. Tilly knew Carrie was angry, but she also suspected the younger girl missed her sister desperately.

CHAPTER 15

"Stop frowning. You'll get lines on your forehead." Becky, Jo's twin sister, teased Tilly as she walked toward her, carrying her son.

"Sorry Becky, I was miles away. How are you? How is young William? He is getting really big already, isn't he?"

Becky shifted her baby onto her other hip. "You can say that again. He's huge. I can't keep him in food. Scott reckons he will soon be able to eat a whole steer."

Tilly reached out her arms to take baby Willie and give him a big cuddle as she laughed at Scott's joke.

"So what were you frowning about? There isn't trouble in paradise, is there? I thought you and Almanzo looked happy."

Tilly shook her head, wondering what to say. She

was happy with Almanzo, but she was worried about Mrs. Morgan and whether the town would ever forget about her and Fiona's arrival in the town. It was hard keeping secrets from Becky. They had bonded the first night Tilly had arrived in Portland. She liked Eva and Jo too, but, out of the three sisters, Becky was her closest friend. "If I tell you, you have to promise not to tell Almanzo."

"Sounds serious," Becky said, her eyes full of concern. "Alright, I promise."

Tilly told Becky what Mrs. Morgan had called her the last time they met in town.

"She still believes myself and Fiona were wrong to return to white civilization. If we had an ounce of self-respect, we should have killed ourselves."

"What? That is just stupid. The Indians rescued you. They didn't take you hostage, and they didn't harm you."

"I know, but Mrs. Morgan and her kind will never believe that."

"Of all the nerve. Wait until I get my hands on that woman. She will wish she was never born."

"No, Becky, you can't say anything. Please. You know if Almanzo hears of it, there'll be trouble. I just have to live with it."

"Tilly Price, you don't have to accept that treatment. Least of all from Mrs. Morgan, that pigheaded excuse of a woman. She deserves to be slapped."

Tilly tried to quell the panic in her stomach. When Becky got annoyed, anything was liable to happen. "Please, Becky. I'm begging you not to say anything. I will deal with Mrs. Morgan if it happens again."

Becky looked her in the eyes. "I won't say a word, but only because you don't want me to. I still think you should put Mrs. Morgan back in her place. After all, she should be keeping her head down. It's her son's fault that Sarah ran away. Well, that's what Jo believes, anyway."

Tilly looked into Becky's face. "And you don't?"

Becky shrugged. "Sarah was always headstrong. I'm not sure who led whom away, to be honest. Edwin Morgan is a weak-minded lily livered pampered only son. I'm not sure he had the guts to suggest eloping."

Tilly gave Willie one last cuddle before she handed him back to his ma. "Do you think Sarah will ever come home?"

Becky looked down at Willie, giving him a quick smile. It vanished when she looked up at Tilly. "As far as that young madam is concerned, she will come back when she needs something and not before. We tried to warn Jo and Rick they were being too soft with her. But they wouldn't listen."

Tilly didn't know what to say. She didn't like to

hear Jo being criticized, but she hadn't been around when Sarah was growing up. Thankfully, she was saved from commenting by the arrival of Becky's husband, Scott.

"There you are. I've been looking for you. Jake and Ruthie want to know if they can ride home by themselves? I told them to ask you." Scott winked at Tilly.

"Ask me? Are you serious? They aren't old enough to do that. They've only just turned seven." Becky let herself get worked up, but then noticed the gleam in Scott's eye. "Wait, you're teasing me, aren't you?"

"Yes, darling, and it works every time. I love your temper. Have I told you that lately?" Scott said, dodging his wife's arm.

"Oh, you," Becky laughed at herself. "I guess I am so predictable. Please tell me you didn't just come over to tease?"

"No, I came to say I think it's time to go home. I don't like the look of those clouds. We have been lucky with the weather today, but I would prefer to get you all home now."

Becky gave Tilly a one armed cuddle as baby Willie was asleep in the other. "I will see you soon and we can talk some more. Now I best go to find Jake and Ruthie. Scott, can you get Anna and Nathan, please?"

"I'll help you look for them," Tilly said. "They're

probably in the kitchen, with Bridget begging her for more cake."

"They know a good cook when they see one," Scott said, giving Tilly a kiss on the cheek. "Tell Almanzo we said goodbye. I'm not sure where he is."

"He's gone to rescue Jo from Becky's children. They wanted to see Aunty Jo, but he thinks it was more like Bridget, as they know she will give them more cookies."

Scott laughed. "Can't blame them, really. I'd sneak off if Bridget gave me cookies, too."

"Come on dear husband, take me home. I can make you cookies tomorrow."

"Thanks, but no thanks, Becky. I need to keep an eye on my waistline." Scott winked at Tilly. It was no secret Becky's talents didn't lie in the kitchen. She was possibly a worse cook than Tilly, and that was saying something.

* * *

Later, when the children were asleep, Tilly found Almanzo on the porch, a book in his lap. He wasn't reading. Instead, he seemed to be far away in his thoughts. Maybe now would be a good time to ask the question that had been plaguing her since Mrs. Newland first mentioned it.

"Almanzo, it was a good party, wasn't it?"

"Yes, darling, everyone had a lot of fun. You were a brilliant hostess."

He moved his book aside before he drew her down to sit on his knee, kissing the back of her neck before putting his arms around her.

"Almanzo, just how close were you and Sarah?"

"Where did that question come from?"

"Someone commented on it. Actually, two people just this week," Tilly said, hating the note of desperation in her voice. She knew her husband loved her, but had he loved Sarah first?

"Tilly, I love you. I married you. You don't have anything to worry about."

"I know that, but I was curious. Did she run off with Morgan because you wouldn't marry her?"

Almanzo laughed and tightened his grip around Tilly. "Sarah had her heart set on Edwin Morgan from the minute Rick told her he was bad news. Unfortunately, she was always testing Jo and Rick. Rick in particular. Something to do with the fact he was going to leave her and Carrie in an orphanage."

Shocked, Tilly stared at him for a few seconds. She couldn't believe that Rick would have done something so heartless. She'd only known him a little while, but still… "He wouldn't have done that. He loved them."

"He did, but at that time, their ma had just died and

he was a single man with no experience of young girls, never mind two who were grieving for their family. They didn't just lose their ma, their two brothers died on the trail too. I guess Rick was at his wit's end."

"So what happened?"

"Jo came to the rescue. From what I heard, they had some fairly strong words about it. After that, Rick and Jo got married and more or less adopted the two girls. And me."

"So you and Sarah were never courting?"

Almanzo lifted her head up so she could see his eyes. "I won't lie to you Tilly. There was a time when I thought that was what I wanted, but Rick helped me realize I was part of this family without having to marry Sarah. I love Sarah the same as I love Carrie. Like two sisters. I love you in a completely different way." As if to demonstrate the truth of his words, he proceeded to show her just how much he loved her.

CHAPTER 16

Sarah woke up feeling groggy. As soon as she lifted her head, she had to hold her hand against her mouth and stumble outside to vomit. Sitting with her head in her hands, she didn't hear Bear until he was right beside her.

"Drink this. It will help. How is the pain?"

Sarah drank eagerly before putting the cup down. She knew she stank to high heaven, but he didn't seem to be offended. "It's better than it was, thank you."

"Do you think you can walk?"

"Yes," Sarah hoped she sounded more confident than she felt.

"Put these on. They will keep your feet more comfortable."

Sarah took the gift he held out to her. The

moccasins had not been worn. "For me?" she looked up into his face in wonder.

"For feet." He replied, obviously thinking she had misunderstood him. She smiled and then put them on her feet. They fit as if they had been made especially for her.

"You will have breakfast and then we must move on. We are too close to town."

"I can eat later. We should go now."

"No, you must be careful. You will hurt the baby."

Shocked, Sarah got to her feet and stood facing him. "How do you know about the baby?"

"I heard you."

"When?"

"When you told the man who hit you. Morgan." The look on Bear's face was difficult for Sarah to read. He looked angry, but she couldn't tell if it was about the baby or her being hit. Or both.

She covered her belly with her hand. Looking back up at Bear, a tear fell from her eye. "He didn't want his own baby."

"He is a stupid man. Now you must eat."

Sarah ate the food Bear had prepared. She wasn't sure what it was and at first her stomach rebelled, but then it settled down. She couldn't eat the whole amount, but he seemed happy with what she did eat.

"I will find horses soon. For now, we walk. You tell me if the pain is bad."

"I will," Sarah said softly, wondering again why this man was taking such good care of her. She could only bring him harm, yet he had risked his life to save her from what was certainly a fate worse than death. And he knew about Edwin. Had he been following her? The thought should have unsettled her but, to her surprise, it didn't. She felt almost comforted, and certainly curious, by the realization.

* * *

Bear matched his pace to hers, although his body wanted to run. He knew what the townsfolk would do to him if they found him. They would never believe he was innocent. Even if she confessed, they would blame the evil man's death on him. To them, he was a savage. The townsfolk would accept a man who beat women and did all kinds of other things, but they would never accept an Indian who was innocent.

He listened closely to her breathing, knowing she was in pain. He was tempted to carry her, but that would slow their progress even more. They would soon be at his camp, where Tala was waiting. Every so often, he doubled back to make sure they were not being followed. So far, their luck held.

"I'm sorry, but I have to rest," she said after a while, her face ashen as he came back toward her. He cursed himself for not noticing how pale she had become. Gently, he picked her up.

"Bear, you can't carry me."

"It is not far to my camp and then we can rest for a while. You are safe. There is nobody following us. For now."

She laid her head against his chest, her sweet smell lingering in his nostrils. Her hair was soft, and it tickled his nose when he bent down to sniff it. He grunted as he shuffled her body closer to his and then walked quickly. He had been honest. There was nobody following them, but yet he couldn't let his guard down. His instincts told him they weren't out of danger yet.

Before too long, they came up to his camp. Tala barked in greeting, causing Miss Sassy to open her eyes. She would have screamed if he didn't clamp a hand over her mouth.

"He is mine. Do not be afraid. He looked after you the first night you stayed in the cave. Do you not remember?"

She shook her head. He laid her gently down on the ground before calling Tala to his side. After greeting the dog for a few minutes, he let the animal sniff Miss Sassy, all the time telling him she was a friend.

"This is Miss Sassy. Miss Sassy, this is Tala. It means wolf."

Her eyes opened wider. "Why do you call me that?"

"It is your name."

"My name is Sarah. Only Walking Tall and his friends call me that name."

"Walking Tall is my friend, too. He is the reason you are here."

CHAPTER 17

Sarah paled, her hand caressing her stomach. "What do you mean 'he is the reason'? Did he send you to find me?"

Bear nodded.

"But why?"

"That is for Walking Tall to explain. I have to take you to his camp."

"I'm not going anywhere until you tell me why."

He smiled, but it didn't light up his eyes. "He told me you were stubborn."

"I am not stubborn."

"Yes, you are. Now, you have no options. No friends, no man. You have nobody but me, yet you still think you can give orders. Make decisions."

"I can. It's up to me where I go and who I go with."

"It is this thinking that got you into trouble. You

did not do what your parents wanted. Your family didn't like the man you were with, did they?"

Sarah gulped. He knew more than she thought he did.

"It doesn't matter what my family thought. That is none of your business."

"It is my business to take you to Walking Tall. This is something I will do."

"Over my dead body."

"I think one dead body is enough."

Sarah gasped. For a minute, she had forgotten about Faulkner. She had killed a man. Despite his actions and his behavior, he was a human being, and she was responsible for his death.

"You need sleep now. Rest while I go hunt. Tala will protect you."

"You can't leave me with that wild animal."

"He is better company than you usually keep."

With that parting remark, Bear was gone. Tala trotted after him, but Bear sent him back to her. Tala whined a couple of times, but gradually he did as ordered and lay down beside Sarah. She was glad of his company, although she would never admit it. Bear hadn't lit a fire. She guessed he was afraid it would lead people to them. It wasn't quite dark yet, but it was rather frightening being alone out here. Having Tala with her was better than nothing.

***

She slept a little, but when Bear didn't come back, she couldn't relax. Every time she closed her eyes, she saw Faulkner's face. She should have stayed in town and told the Sheriff what had happened. But would he have believed her? She shuddered when she remembered the lynching the previous month. A man had been accused of stabbing another miner. Before the sheriff could do anything, the man had a rope around his neck, was dragged to the edge of town and hanged. There was no trial. She didn't know if he was guilty or not, but nobody seemed to care. That was how it was done in mining towns. They didn't wait for the Judge to arrive. In the case of Indians, they wouldn't have waited for anyone.

Tala straightened. His ears pinned forward. He nudged her a little, whining softly. She rubbed his fur and then said, "go."

Amazingly, he licked her hand and then ran. Soon he returned, running rings around Bear who was carrying a carcass of some kind in one hand and a bundle in the other.

"Are you ready to move on?"

"Yes. But don't you need to rest?"

"No time. I do not feel comfortable being this near town. We need to put distance between us and them."

She stood up, ignoring the pain in her side.

"Which way?" she asked.

"We go this way. Have you some water?"

"Yes, I filled this up by the creek."

"I told you to stay where you were." He scowled at her.

She wasn't about to let him think she was afraid of him. "I was thirsty. I was careful. Tala looked out for me."

His face cracked into a smile. "You made friends."

"You were right. He is better company than anyone else I have been near."

Instead of being angry, Bear threw back his head and laughed.

"Walking Tall said you had spirit. He was not joking."

Sarah itched to slap his face for laughing at her, but instead she turned on her heel and marched off. He called her a couple of times, but she ignored him. Then he laughed again.

"What is so funny?"

"You might want to walk this way. Otherwise, you will be back in town in no time."

In frustration, she balled her fists so tight her nails bit into her palms. She could have screamed. But instead, she marched back and moved in the direction he indicated, all the time listening to him laugh behind her.

"Do you mind?" her frosty tone did nothing to wipe the grin from his face. Instead, he laughed even more.

"It is good to laugh. It helps relieve anger. You should try it sometime."

He moved ahead of her and she stuck her tongue out at his back. She stumbled slightly, a good reminder she should concentrate on the terrain underfoot. The moccasins were so comfortable that if she wasn't careful, she could trip over one of the many tree roots. The forest became denser as they moved away from the town, something she found comforting. There was less chance of them being followed.

CHAPTER 18

*B*ear walked slightly ahead of her, thinking she needed some privacy. He didn't walk fast, as he could see she was struggling. He was tempted to carry her, but that would only slow them down further.

"You must tell me when it becomes too painful to continue."

"I'm fine."

It was obvious she was lying as she spoke through gritted teeth, but he pretended to believe her. He'd been honest when he said they were far too near town for comfort. Even though he didn't think anyone had seen them with Faulkner, there was always a chance someone had. It was better for everyone if the town became a distant memory. And Morgan was still around somewhere. Bear hadn't followed him, so he didn't know which direction that man had taken.

He heard her hiss of pain. Putting his bundles in one arm, he whisked her into his arms. She protested slightly, but obviously lacked the energy to fight him hard.

"Try to rest a little. We will not go much farther. There are some caves up ahead. They will shelter us for a while."

"Will they not trace us to them?"

"Maybe if they could find my tracks. But the white man tends to be afraid of mountain lions. They like these caves."

Her heart beat faster against his chest, making him curse his stupidity.

"You do not have anything to worry about. I will protect you."

She didn't look at him.

"Miss Sassy?"

"Please stop calling me that. My name is Sarah."

"Sarah, trust me. I am on your side."

She looked into his eyes and he saw a flicker of trust. Or maybe that is just what he wanted to see. His own heart beat faster and he knew that had nothing to do with any dangerous animals. Except maybe for the woman in his arms. She had a hold on his heart already. And the thought terrified him.

He moved as quickly as he could, despite the extra weight. His shoulder ached a little, but he ignored it. He kept an eye on Tala, who scampered around their feet, knowing the dog would sense any danger before he did.

After cresting a mountain of rocks, he found what he'd been looking for. Their shelter.

"We are here, Sarah. Wake up."

She opened her eyes, then seemed to realize she was still in his arms. Her cheeks turned a pretty shade of pink. She looked vulnerable, and he wanted to protect her.

"Please, let me down. I'm fine now."

He let her down gently. Good thing too, because as soon as he put her on her own feet, she swayed and lost consciousness. It was only then that he spotted the blood. She was injured and hadn't told him.

"Sarah? Wake up." He lay her gently on the ground, but she didn't wake up. He rushed to lay the furs down and then carefully he undressed her in a bid to locate the injury. She was bleeding quite heavily. Oh no, the baby.

He went to the stream to get water to clean her. When the cold water touched her skin, she regained consciousness. He washed her gently and dried her as she slipped away again. He lit a small fire and prayed hard for the strength to help her. Tala whined and kept pawing her to wake up, but she didn't.

"Leave her boy. She needs to rest. She will be better soon."

He hoped he was right.

* * *

Sarah slept for hours. He checked on her a few times and was relieved to see the bleeding seemed to have stopped. He moved her into the cave, after making up a more comfortable bed with grass covered by one of his furs. He cleared the immediate area of leaves and twigs, just in case they hid snakes or scorpions. Then, he lit a small fire and began roasting the animal he had caught earlier. He also boiled water in a small can that used to belong to his sister. Using the warm water, he washed Sarah again. He knew the danger now was not from the loss of the child, but from the loss of blood. He took the risk she would wake up alone and went hunting for some medicinal herbs. His stock was running low and there was one of the women of the tribe used to make blood stronger. He ordered Tala to keep watch over Sarah.

He wasn't gone long, and she was still sleeping when he returned. He ate alone but couldn't eat much. He was terrified she would die. Why was she sleeping so long? Was the baby the reason why she had been so desperate to stay with Edwin Morgan? He knew in the white woman's world, to have a babe outside of marriage was a bad thing. How could he have thought she was just too stubborn to acknowledge she had made a mistake? The poor girl must have been terrified. He didn't know her family, but from what Walking Tall said, they sounded like good people. Would they have cared if she came home with a baby and no husband?

CHAPTER 19

Sarah floated in and out of consciousness. She wasn't sure where she was, but she was warm and felt safe. For the first time in a long time, she was totally relaxed. All she wanted to do was sleep. She was dimly aware of someone looking after her, washing her down and trying to feed her, but she wasn't hungry. Her stomach cramped, but when she drank, the pains went. She fell back asleep into a dreamless world.

Gradually she woke for longer periods of time and began to become aware of her existence. She was lying under a pile of rather smelly furs. It was quite comfortable apart from the smell, but even that was becoming more bearable. Her stomach hurt. She put her hand down to stroke it before realizing she was totally naked. She grabbed the furs closer. Where were her clothes? Who had undressed her? She edged up in the makeshift bed.

She realized she was in some sort of cave. She closed her eyes, trying to remember the events of the last few days, but there was nothing. She felt around the ground for her clothes but found only dirt. Then a dog licked her face. It seemed really happy to see her. She pushed it away, but it barked and insisted on licking her again. Then it went to the opening of the cave, barked some more, and came back to lick her face and hands again.

"You are awake. Good. Tala was worried."

"You? You brought me here. Undressed me?" her voice wavered, but his facial expression didn't change. He certainly didn't look embarrassed. "Why?"

Her stomach did a double somersault at the look on his face. "What?"

"Sarah, do you not remember leaving town?"

"No."

"Or anything else?"

"No, you're scaring me. What happened?"

He bent down and took one of her hands in his. The expression on his face was a mixture of tenderness and pity. She was suddenly very afraid. "You're scaring me."

"I am very sorry, but you lost your baby."

"What? How do you know? What do you mean? How could I?"

She snapped her hand away and covered her stomach with both hands. Somehow, she knew he was telling the truth, but how could she not know? How could something like that happen and she be unaware of it?

"Morgan kicked you viciously and then, with your work and the walk and everything, it must have been too much. You were bleeding for a long time. Nothing I could do worked. It wouldn't stop."

"You mean it was you who nursed me? Washed me?" her cheeks heated as she closed her eyes, trying to remember. But the last few days were pure darkness.

"Maybe it is better you do not remember. You are young and strong. It looks like you are recovering. I was worried you were going to die, too."

"Too?"

"Do you remember why we had to leave town?"

She shook her head, not able to stop the tear from sliding down her face.

"Faulkner threatened you. He wanted you to work off debts of Morgan's. He pulled his gun on us and you hit him with a rock."

"I killed him," she said, sounding dreamlike. "I remember now. I killed a man. No wonder my baby died. It's punishment for what I did. You should leave me here."

"Sarah, stop it. You didn't do anything but protect yourself and me. Nobody ever tried to protect me like that before."

"But my..." she couldn't bring herself to say the word.

"I am sorry about what happened to you. I wish I had known that first night. I may have used the wrong herbs. Maybe my medicine caused it."

She couldn't believe this kind man was blaming himself for what had happened to her. He had saved her life.

"No, you didn't do anything but help me. I still don't understand why, but I am very grateful to you. Edwin would have killed me for saying no to Faulkner. He didn't want the baby, anyway. He..." she couldn't go on as the tears came. She rocked back and forth inside the furs. He came closer, but she didn't move. She didn't react when he put his arms around her and drew her toward his chest. She lay her head against him, listening to his heartbeat as she cried and cried. Not just for her baby, but for herself.

CHAPTER 20

It took a while for the tears to run dry and only then did she remember she was naked and leaning against a stranger's chest. It didn't matter the stranger had already seen her body. That was different. She'd been unconscious. Blushing, she gathered the furs closer around her.

"Thank you," she murmured, too embarrassed to look at him.

"You should eat," he said. "You need to build up strength for our journey. It will take many days."

"Where are we going?"

"I will take you to Walking Tall's camp. He will return you to your parents."

"No," she shouted, panic making her voice louder than she intended. He drew away from her. "Sorry, I didn't mean to shout. But I can't go home. Not now, not like this. My parents will be so ashamed of me."

"Your parents love you. They will forgive you."

"How do you know?"

He looked at her. She caught the sadness in his eyes before he looked away. "It is what I have been told. Now I must find food and you should get dressed. I washed your clothes, and they dried by the fire. They should be ready."

She couldn't do anything but mumble her thanks. She had never known a man to wash anything. Even her uncle Rick, who was amazing on every level, didn't wash clothes. Before Jo had come along, he had paid a lady on the wagon train to do her and Carrie's laundry. She got dressed quickly as Bear went to cook. Her clothes were not only clean and dry but smelled lovely, too.

She cleaned up the little cave as best she could before making her way to the fire where Bear was cooking. She didn't offer to help, as her cooking skills couldn't match his. She ruffled Tala's fur absentmindedly as she watched Bear cook.

"Why haven't we met before? Have you lived with Walking Tall for long?"

"Many years I have stayed at his camp."

"But you never came down to Portland?"

"No."

She sensed there was a reason why, but he seemed hesitant to talk about it. She held her tongue for a bit, but eventually curiosity got the better of her. "Why?"

"Why what?"

"Why didn't you come down to Portland? Walking Tall brought many braves and their families down to see my brother, Almanzo. Well, he is not really my brother. My uncle Rick and his wife Jo adopted him on the trail."

"I know Almanzo."

She couldn't tell whether he liked Almanzo or not; his expression was closed.

"Did we meet when Jo went to help the Indians on the trail?"

"I saw Jo working, but she did not bring young girls with her. She came with another lady. Jo is a very clever healer. Walking Tall's women gave her moccasins as a gift."

"Yes, they did. She still has them. Or at least she did." Sarah looked into the distance, wondering how Jo and Rick were. She missed her family.

"Why did you not learn healing gifts from her?" Bear asked as he handed Sarah a plate.

"How do you know I didn't?" she countered.

"You didn't help the young boy when he asked."

Shame colored her face. So he had seen her refuse Johnny.

"How long were you watching me?"

"Some weeks, maybe a month."

"That long? You have been spying on me and you never let on you were there?"

He didn't flinch at her tone. He just stared at her. "What would you have done if you knew?"

"I would have told you to go home," she replied honestly.

"So?"

"What do you mean 'so'?"

"I am not your man or a dog. I do not go just because you say so."

"You have no right." Her anger at his presumption made her tone sharper than she intended.

"I have every reason to follow you. I was asked to do it and I owe a large debt to the person who asked me. Your parents wanted to know you were safe."

"My parents sent you?" Wild hope filled Sarah. She could go home. If they had sent Indians looking for her, they must really want her to come back to Portland. Tears pricked her eyes.

"I do not know if they know I am here. Walking Tall sent me. He is concerned about your parents and you."

Sarah let the plate fall. Tala demolished the contents, but she didn't care.

"Why is Walking Tall worried about my parents? What is wrong with them?"

"I do not know. I did not ask. Walking Tall is Chief now. He says do, and I go do."

"Oh. That is so annoying."

"What is? I respect my elders and betters. But I can see you find that concept strange."

His knowing tone irked her, although she knew he was right. She hadn't shown much respect for anyone. Not her parents, or even herself. Still, she felt compelled to defend herself. "What is that supposed to mean? How dare you judge me? You don't know me."

He regarded her silently for so long she didn't think he was going to answer.

Then he stood up, taking her plate with his. "No, I do not know you. But I have seen enough to see you are spoiled and badly behaved. You think only of yourself. Good night."

And he was gone, leaving her speechless behind him. She opened her mouth to retaliate, but what could she say? He was right.

CHAPTER 21

Bear stomped off, furious with himself for losing his temper. She had been through enough, and here he was judging her. He had no right to do that. But she had gotten under his skin in a way no woman had ever done. He had nearly lost his reason when she was unresponsive to his medicine. When he was away from her, he found himself missing her smile and the way she fidgeted with her hair. He was angry because a woman like her had chosen a man like Morgan. But what good was it doing, taking his anger out on her? Hadn't she paid a high enough price?

He kicked some stones as he walked, but it didn't help. He needed to cool off. He was tempted to strip and go for a swim, but he didn't have time for that. Not now. It was too dangerous to leave her alone. It didn't seem like anyone was looking for them, but what if she got sick again? What if the bleeding came back, and he wasn't nearby? Not that she was likely to ask him for help. He had behaved like a pig. Walking Tall cared for Sarah. Bear knew this from the stories his friend had told over the years. It wasn't just because she was part of Almanzo's extended family. Walking Tall seemed to see something in Sarah he admired. Bear sat and thought about this for a while. What was it? She was stubborn, that much was obvious. But he supposed she was also brave. It hadn't been easy to wait on her own in a mining village where single women were rarer than hen's teeth. She had gotten a job too, a way to support herself and her baby. He gritted his teeth. Maybe he had been wrong about her. Had she been afraid of going with the boy to help him? That was understandable if she was thinking of her child. It was very easy to sit on the outside and judge someone else. But until you walked in that person's shoes, you didn't know what they were dealing with. That was the message Snow Maiden had tried to instill in him. But he hadn't listened then, and it seemed he still hadn't gotten the message. His sister had been sweet and kind hearted whereas he seemed to have a stone for a heart. Why else would he orally attack a woman who had just lost her child?

Tala's barking alerted him that something was

wrong. Drawing his knife, he curbed his instinct to run back to the cave and padded stealthily up to it. If Tala was barking due to strangers, he wanted the element of surprise on his side.

* * *

Sarah had sat at the dwindling fire, watching in the direction Bear had taken. She should be angry at the way he had spoken to her, but she wasn't. How could she be? He was right. She had been selfish from the very start. Rick and Jo had tried to tell her Edwin wasn't the man for her. Rick had agreed to them courting, but she couldn't wait a year. She knew now that her uncle had probably hoped that a year would have given her time to see Edwin's true colors. But would it have been enough?

She knew Almanzo and the rest of her family hated the Morgans, and with good reason. That family was horrible, always making disgusting comments about other people. Mrs. Morgan had even made disparaging remarks about Tilly and Fiona, suggesting they shouldn't have returned from captivity. Not that the Indians were responsible for their abduction. The tribe had actually saved their lives, but the truth wasn't of interest to Mrs. Morgan. Why couldn't Sarah have seen the apple didn't fall far from the tree? Edwin shared all of his mother's opinions in addition to even more unsavory ones he dreamed up for himself. How could he suggest she would work off his debts by selling her body to Faulkner? She let a tear slide down her face, then realized Tala was growling beside her.

"He'll be back soon, Tala. Settle down."

But the dog wouldn't settle. He kept baring his teeth.

"What's wrong?" Sarah picked up a stone, but even as she did, she knew it would be no match for whatever Tala was growling at. Tala started barking louder. Sarah caught a glimpse of what had alerted him. It wasn't the men from town as she had suspected, but something much worse.

CHAPTER 22

"Tala, come here, boy. Don't go near it, he'll hurt you." She made a grab for Tala, but he evaded her. Instead, he ran toward the cat, barking loudly, but she swiped him away with her vicious claws. Whimpering pitifully, Tala flew through the air to land heavily on his side. Sarah watched in horror as he tried to get to his feet but couldn't. The cat looked from her to the dog and back before making its way toward Tala.

Without even thinking, Sarah threw the stone in her hand at the cat. Silently, she thanked Almanzo for all his lessons growing up. In her determination to throw like a boy, she had developed a good aim. The stone hit the cat in her flank, making her hiss with anger. Sarah picked up some more stones and threw them as she made her way toward the fire. The remains of their roasted meal were beside it. She picked up the food and threw it at the cat. Sarah hoped that would satisfy her, but no. The cat sniffed it and walked past.

It came toward her, but slowly, as if wondering what was the best way to attack. Sarah racked her brains trying to remember what she knew about these big cats. But adrenaline drowned out her memory. Tala got to his feet and dragged himself toward the cat, barking like mad. She winced as the cat turned to look at him.

"No," she screamed, but before she could do anything, a knife whizzed through the air and hit the cat right in the chest.

"Sarah, get to the cave now. Move."

But Sarah couldn't move. Her gaze was stuck on the cat, hissing at Bear.

"Sarah go. I have to get Tala. Take a fire log with you."

Sarah broke out of her trance and grabbed a lit log, then walked slowly backward to the cave. The cat didn't pay her any attention. She watched, horrified, as Bear moved slowly toward the injured dog, calling for him to come. Tala tried, but it was obvious he was too badly hurt. The cat snarled as Bear grew closer. Sarah couldn't just watch. She threw the fire log at the cat, screaming at Bear to grab Tala and run. The fire log didn't hit the cat, but it was enough to scare her off. She escaped back into the bushes, leaving Bear free to carry Tala and run back to Sarah.

"Don't you ever do as you are told?"

"Is he okay? Will he die?"

"Get the water and get into the cave. That cat will be back. My knife didn't do sufficient damage. A wounded wild animal is more dangerous."

Sarah didn't doubt that. She ran to grab the water and another lit stick from the fire. She figured they would need a fire in the cave. Bear waited until she was safe before following after her, Tala cradled in his arms. He lay the injured animal down gently.

"He was so brave trying to defend me. She used her claws." Sarah spoke through the tears running down her face.

"We need to wash away the blood and see how bad his injuries are. Can you do that while I light the fire? I want to put a fire between us and that cat."

"Yes." Her voice shook as much as her hands, but she was determined to help the dog who had saved her life. Tala whimpered, his heart beating very fast. As gently as she could, she washed away the blood. Some of the cuts were deep, the blood pooling back up as soon as she wiped it away. "I think he needs stitches."

* * *

BEAR USED the fire log to light the fire. Thankfully, he had stacked up some firewood just in case they had to go deeper into the cave system. He kicked himself for leaving Sarah and Tala alone. What had he been thinking?

Only once he was satisfied the fire was big enough to keep the cat away, he turned his attention to Tala. Sarah was right. Some of the cuts were deep enough to need stitches. He had a small sewing kit in his bags. A maiden at the camp had insisted he take it with him. She had traded a fur for it with some white women who had come by on the trail. He handed it to Sarah.

"Can you do it?"

She looked at Tala and then up to him. "I can try. I haven't sewn up an animal before, but Jo and her sisters tried to teach me how to do needlework." She stared at the poor dog with tears in her eyes. "I'll need you to hold him still."

Bear nodded, trying to hold back his own tears as he watched the little dog whimper in pain. He stroked Tala again and again as Sarah worked on the stitches. He made sure to hold Tala's mouth away from Sarah's hands. He didn't think the dog would bite her, but you never knew with an injured wild animal.

CHAPTER 23

Sarah worked carefully but quickly, all the time worrying about the little dog. He had been so brave trying to protect her. She looked up at one point to see Bear staring at her, and the expression in his eyes took her breath away. She quickly returned to the job at hand. She didn't want to make a fool of herself. After what Bear had said earlier, before the cat attacked, he had made it perfectly clear what a low opinion of her he held.

Usually she didn't care what people thought, but Bear wasn't people. He was a sweet, kind, and sensitive man whom she guessed had been through some difficult times. She wondered why Walking Tall had never encouraged him to come to Portland. He usually brought as many of the Indian braves as he could. He was as keen on fostering a good relationship with the whites as Almanzo and Scott were with the Indians. But then, not everyone felt the same. You only had to look at Edwin and his family for proof of that.

"You are scowling. Do you think you cannot do it?"

She jumped when he spoke, having forgotten he was beside her.

"No, that's not it. Almost done. I was just thinking about something else. I think these will keep, but we have to find a way to stop him from biting at the stitches. And we have to keep the wounds clean."

Bear stroked the dog, who had fallen into a deeply deserved sleep. "Any ideas on how we do that?" Bear asked Sarah.

"No, not really. I guess we may have to teach him not to fuss with his stitches. We can see when he wakes up." She lifted the pup gently on the fur blanket and covered him. "I should wash my hands." She moved toward the cave's exit, but Bear's hand came out to stop her.

"You can't go outside. The cat may be still there or she may have attracted others. Stay here. I will get water."

"But…"

"I will be safe."

He was gone before she could say anything else. He wasn't gone long, but the seconds seemed like hours. She sat beside Tala, her hand on his chest, making sure his heart was still beating. She didn't rate his chances of recovering. For such a young animal, the injuries he had sustained were too many. Still, she prayed. She didn't stop to think that it was silly to pray for a dog. Instead, she wondered where Bear had gotten him. Sarah could see he wasn't a pure wolf-hound, but seemed to be a mix of a wolf and some other type of dog. Every time she heard a noise, she looked up, but there was no sign of Bear.

She looked around the cave, but, other than a few stones, there was nothing to use as a weapon. What if the cat killed Bear and then came back to the cave? She closed her eyes and prayed harder.

CHAPTER 24

Jo twisted back and forth in the bed. Sarah was in trouble; she could tell. Every night for the last week or so, she had nightmares about her adopted daughter.

Bridget knocked on the door before coming in with her breakfast. She had insisted Jo stay in bed, at least until she ate something.

"Lord, but you look pale today. I think I best get the doc over to check on you."

"I don't need the doctor. Just some sleep."

Bridget didn't look convinced.

"Bridget, do you believe you can pick up messages from someone else, even if they are far away?"

Bridget's eyes widened, making Jo feel stupid for saying anything. She would end up in a hospital for mad people at this rate.

"Do you mean like the second sight?"

Bridget crossed herself, but Jo doubted she even realized what she was doing.

"I don't know. No, I don't think so. I just can't help feeling Sarah is in trouble."

Bridget put her hands on her hips. "Of course she's in trouble. She picked that eejit Edwin Morgan. Don't anyone need any second sight to see that he is a bad one?"

"This is more than that, Bridget. Why am I getting these feelings now? She's been gone for months."

"Maybe it's the baby coming? Your mind could be looking for other things to think about rather than the pain of childbirth."

Jo looked at Bridget, who only then seemed to realize what she had said. She put her hand over her mouth before apologizing.

"What am I saying, Jo? I didn't mean that. Of course, the birth will be fine. Oh my goodness, I need to stop talking." Bridget tried to cover her embarrassment by making up the bed and picking up items of clothing.

"Bridget, stop. I've had other children. I know what to expect. Still, if I ever need cheering up, remind me not to ask you."

She smiled at the Irish woman who had brightened up her days, especially since she lost Rick and Sarah.

"Jo, do you want me to go into town and see if Mrs. Morgan has heard from her boy?"

"You hate that woman," Jo replied, surprised that Bridget had offered.

"I love you more. Would it ease your mind to know?" Bridget's expression suggested Jo was better off not knowing anything about Sarah and Edwin. The reality might be worse than her fears.

"No, don't say anything. But thank you for offering. I just wish there was a way to tell Sarah she could come home. I don't care whether she married Morgan or not. She should be here. Especially if there's to be a war."

Bridget patted her hand and fluffed up her pillows. "You stop worrying about things you got no control over, Miss Joh—I mean, Jo. Now you eat your breakfast. Then you need to get some sleep because you won't be getting much when that little baby is here. Do you hear me?"

"I think Tilly might hear you from her house, Bridget. There's no need to shout at me. I'm not deaf," Jo grumbled.

"No, but you aren't good at listening, either. You need to look after you and that baby. Everything else can wait. Once the baby has come and you two are doing fine, we'll work on getting Sarah home. You trust me, Miss Johanna."

"Bridget, you promised to call me Jo."

"Not when you're acting like this, Miss Johanna. I think I should get your mam over here to talk to you."

Jo knew she was defeated. "You win. I promise I will rest. Please don't tell Ma. You know how much she fusses, and I can't bear that. I'll even eat, look."

Jo shoveled the food into her mouth despite her lack of appetite. The last thing she needed was her mother to come and stay. Much as she loved Della Thompson, her mother would fuss and fuss worse than Bridget did.

Bridget stayed while she ate and then took the breakfast dishes away. Jo closed her eyes and pretended to sleep until the door closed. Then she opened them. How could she find Sarah? The outbreak of war would surely make it more difficult to move around the country. She didn't know how bad things would get. Nobody did. She shut her eyes, trying to keep away the thoughts of her loved ones having to go and fight. Bridget was right. She should concentrate on her baby now and stop worrying about the rest.

CHAPTER 25

Sarah had counted how many steps it took to pace around the cave and back again before Bear returned. He handed her the water pail, splashing a little as he did so.

"You took your time. I was so scared."

He didn't answer, so she washed her hands quickly as he went to check on Tala. The dog had whimpered a few times but now seemed to be sleeping again. Bear sat down, and she noticed something about his movement was off.

"What happened? Are you hurt?"

He didn't answer, but leaned his side against the wall of the cave. She caught a grimace of pain cross his face.

"Bear, talk to me."

"The cat is dead. I tracked it and killed it."

"Oh, thank goodness. I was so scared. You hear such horrible stories." She knew she was babbling, but had a hard time stopping herself. "Bear?"

He moaned and slumped forward. She screamed at the sight of blood pouring from a cut on his back. He was hurt. She had to get a hold of herself. She moved closer to examine the wound. He tried to stop her, but he didn't seem to have the strength. She moved his shirt out of the way, gasping with horror when she saw the scars on his back. Thin white lines crisscrossed the entire surface as far as she could see. He'd been badly hurt before. But she couldn't deal with that now. She had to stop the bleeding. She turned away from him as she yanked up her skirt to tear strips from her petticoats.

He was the one who had washed and dressed her, so it was a bit late for modesty anyhow. Wetting the cloth, she sponged the wound as gently as she could. He tensed, but didn't make a sound. The blood wouldn't stop. The cloth and the water turned red.

"It's deep. I think I have to stitch it like I did with Tala."

"No, too deep. You will have to burn it."

Sarah bit back the bile that threatened to escape. He couldn't be serious.

"Sarah, you have to do this. If Walking Tall were here, he would do it."

"I'm not Walking Tall. I've never burned anyone before. I can't hurt you like that."

"If you don't, I will lose the power of my arm. I may even die. You have to. I cannot reach the wound." Bear stared at her. "I beg you. Please do it."

"But what about the pain? I could kill you."

"You will not."

Sarah wished she had his confidence. She prayed hard for another solution, but nothing came to mind.

"Sarah, please. You have to do it now before I lose more blood."

She summoned all of her resolve before nodding. "Okay then. What do I do?"

"Boil some water and clean my knife. Then you need to hold the metal part over the fire until it is hot. Do not wait until it glows red."

She wanted to vomit, but had to fight that instinct. He needed her to be strong. "What then?"

"You need to hold the hot blade to the wound. Not for long, a couple of seconds at a time." Then, perhaps noting her hesitation, he added, "You can do this."

Sarah picked up the blade—it was covered in blood. Her hands shook so much she dropped it. Cursing under her breath, she picked it up again.

"Sarah, you can do this. I believe you can."

Looking into his eyes gave her strength. She pushed her shoulders back, took the knife, and set it on a stone by the fire. Then she took more water and put it on the fire to boil. She tore more strips off for Bear to press against the wound to try to stop the flow of blood. Then she looked for a small stick. When the water had boiled, she washed the knife. She didn't dry it, but let it dry over the heat of the flames. She came back to him, her eyes wide. He nodded at her, taking the bandage away from the wound, which immediately poured with blood again. She gave him the stick to bite on. At his nod, she took a deep breath and held the blade to the wound for a couple of seconds. The smell was as horrifying as the hissing sound of the metal blade against his scorched flesh. The grinding noise of his teeth made her look at his face. Pain-filled eyes stared back at her before he squeezed them shut.

Seeing he was in agony, she almost stopped, but he opened his eyes and motioned for her to do it again. Tears flowed down her face, but she did it a second time. And then a third. Surely that was enough. She took the blade and put it back in the boiling water to clean. Turning to Bear, she gulped at the look of pain in his eyes.

She gently removed the stick from his mouth. "You should rest. Shall I bandage up the wound?"

"No, leave it open. Tomorrow, salve."

She watched as he lay down on his stomach, leaving his upper back and shoulder open to the air.

She covered his legs with one of the furs. She didn't know much about doctoring, but Jo was always worried about shock. "You need to stay warm. I will add to the fire."

"Thank you," he whispered.

She checked on Tala before adding more fuel to the fire. She had spotted a couple of mint flowers at the entrance to the cave. She gathered them and added them to the flames, hoping it would cover the smell of burning flesh. She checked on Bear, but he was out cold. Tala whined a little. She moved the dog closer to his owner, and it seemed to help settle him a bit. Then, drawing the other fur around her shoulders, she sat near the fire. Only then did she let the tears come. Not only for what she had just done, but for the marks she had seen on Bear's back. How could anyone do that to another human being?

CHAPTER 26

It was a long night. She kept checking Bear to make sure he didn't develop a fever. She gave him regular sips of water, but he declined food. That was a good thing, as they had very little left. When it was light, she would have to go and find some. But how? She should have listened more to Walking Tall and Almanzo when they tried to teach her how to survive away from town. She knew a little, but wasn't sure it would be enough to keep two adults going over a few days. And she didn't know how long Bear would be laid up. What would she do if he developed a fever? Could she get to another town and get a doctor? She didn't even know if a doctor would treat him. The doctor back at the mining town wouldn't. And she didn't have any money to offer a doctor, anyway. The little she had saved had been in one of the bundles Edwin had taken. No doubt he had it spent already on beer and whiskey.

She kept adding logs to the fire to keep it glowing bright. Bear had killed that one cat, but would the scent of blood attract others? She didn't want to take any risks. Finally, she lay down on the fur beside the fire and let her eyes close. She was just going to take a quick nap before she had to check on Bear again.

* * *

He gritted his teeth in agony as the pain pierced his body. The previous night had been bad when she'd put the hot blade against his shoulder, but the next morning was worse. Now his whole back was beating a tune in pain. He rolled to try to get to his feet but, despite several attempts, it was useless. He was too weak from loss of blood. Closing his eyes, he relived the last moments of the cat's life. He'd been incredibly lucky. She wasn't as badly injured as he had first thought. She was a brave fighter, but in the end, had been no match for his strength. Still, she hadn't died without a fight. His shoulder was a painful reminder of that.

He had no idea how he'd managed to get back to the cave. He'd known he couldn't leave Sarah alone, that she would be frightened. And she had reason to be. The cat must have a family close by to have fought as fiercely as she had. Bear guessed she had been protecting her pack.

* * *

Sarah could tell he was awake. She filled a cup with water and moved over to where he lay.

"How are you feeling?"

"Very good," he replied.

She smiled at his attempt to stop her worrying. "Bear, what can I do to help? You said something last night about caring for the wound."

"I will have to gather some herbs to stop the wound going bad, but maybe tomorrow. How is Tala?"

"He seems a little better. He's been trying to nibble at his stitches." She lifted the dog gently and placed him near Bear's face. The animal licked his cheek, making him smile. Sarah's heart leaped in her chest as she witnessed the love the two shared for each other. It was silly, but she felt she was imposing.

"I can go look for herbs if you tell me what to look for."

"No, don't. It is best you do not go outside."

His tone scared her. "Why?"

"I do not believe the cat was alone. I think she was protecting her family. I would prefer you stay here."

"Are you worried I'll get hurt?" What had made her say that? But still, she waited for an answer.

"Walking Tall would not be happy if anything happened to you. Please do not leave." His face was like a blank mask. She couldn't tell what he was thinking.

"I won't." She struggled not to acknowledge that his answer had hurt her. He didn't care about her after all. He was just concerned about taking her back to Walking Tall. And who could blame him, either? He hadn't seen a good picture of her.

CHAPTER 27

Jo held onto the side of the bed as the pains cut through her. They were coming faster now. Where was Bridget? She tried not to scream, as she didn't want to scare the children.

"Morning," Bridget sang as she finally entered Jo's room. "Oh my God, has it started?"

Jo nodded as she panted through another contraction.

"Get into bed. I will go put water on to boil."

Jo ignored the suggestion to get into bed. She would be better walking for now. That had helped when the twins had been born. Rick had held her hand right up until the midwife shooed him away. Rick. Why wasn't he here? She gritted her teeth as another pain wracked her body.

Bridget had gone, she suspected she'd sent Carrie

for Tilly and Almanzo. But it was too late. The baby would be here before the midwife or doctor reached them from town. She panted again, trying to remember what she had done when giving birth to the twins. How she wished Della were here.

Just then, the bedroom door opened, and her ma walked in. Jo couldn't believe her eyes.

"I had a funny feeling you would be needing me today. Thank goodness for the sixth sense, or whatever your granny would have called it. Walk now, girl, keep walking. How far apart are the pains?"

"About five minutes now and getting closer," Jo managed to squeak. Her ma gave her some water to drink before turning down the bedcovers. She then busied herself making up the bed with the old sheets Jo had set aside for this day.

"Do you think it will be a boy or a girl?"

"I don't care, Ma, so long as it's healthy."

"I'm sure it will be. God knows you had enough to contend with this past year," Della murmured.

Jo didn't respond. The pains gripped her again, and her body wanted to push. She let her ma help her onto the bed. Bridget arrived with some hot water and towels, but ran as soon as it looked like the baby was coming. Jo grimaced in pain but couldn't stop herself from exchanging a look with her ma.

"Good thing I came calling; otherwise, you would have been having this baby alone."

"Bridget would have stayed. You here. Doesn't have to." Jo couldn't complete her sentences, but barked out bits between the pain. Her ma understood. Jo looked at Della with gratitude. Her ma could be scared stiff, but you would never tell from her face. She faced life every day in the same way—come rain or shine, she was always smiling or at least trying to. And now she smiled down at Jo as she washed the sweat from her face.

"Thought of any names yet?"

Jo couldn't answer. She had thought about names, but she wasn't saying anything until the baby was in her arms. She wondered if it would be a boy. She knew Rick had wanted a son. Not that he didn't love his daughters—of course he did—but all men wanted a boy to carry on their name. To keep their land in the family.

She gritted her teeth and pushed and pushed until the baby arrived. Why wasn't it crying? She used her last remaining strength to push herself up in the bed. "Ma, what's wrong?"

Her ma wasn't smiling but stood staring at the bundle as if in shock.

"Ma, what's wrong?" Jo cried out, unaware of how loud she was until Bridget came running. Her friend looked from Jo to Della and back at the baby. Without a word, she picked up the baby, held it face down by the legs, and gave it a resounding slap on the backside. Jo screamed at Bridget to leave her baby alone, but Bridget ignored her. She examined the baby quickly before giving it another slap, and the baby cried in protest. Tears streaming down her face, Bridget handed the little one over to Jo.

"Seems your son is as stubborn as his ma."

Jo examined the now screaming bundle in her arms. Her baby was perfect. A boy. Rick had a son. A hungry one too, if his open mouth jutting at her chest was anything to go by.

"Bridget, where did you learn to do that?"

"I grew up on a farm in the middle of nowhere. My ma had a baby just like yours. I saw an old woman do it, but I never tried it before myself."

Jo didn't care about her qualifications or experience. Bridget had saved her baby, and she would never forget it. "Thank God you were here, Bridget. Without you, we would have lost him."

"No, you would have done the same once you realized you didn't have a choice. The woman in Ireland who came to help my mam give birth said the crying helped the baby breathe." Bridget cooed at the baby before she went for some hot water for Jo's bath.

"Once you're all clean and tidy, I will get you a nice cup of tea."

"You might get me something stronger," Jo's mom said.

"Now, Miss Della, don't be having me on. I know you're not one for the hard stuff."

Jo giggled. She had never seen her ma with an alcoholic drink but, judging by the look on her face, she could have done with one today.

"He is beautiful, Jo." Her ma beamed in approval.

"He's a little angel."

"What are you going to call him, or should I guess?"

"Richard, but Richie for short. There was only one Rick," Jo said before dissolving into tears. "Oh Ma, it's so unfair. He would have loved a son."

"He loves his son as much as he loves you and the girls. He is holding you all close to his heart, Johanna. Never forget that. Just because you can't see him doesn't mean he isn't here."

Jo tried to control her sobs. She knew her ma meant well, but she really needed to see Rick. Just one more time.

"Now give me my new grandson, and I will bathe him and put a diaper on him while you have a bath. Then you need to go back to bed and rest."

"I don't want to give him up just yet, Ma."

"I know you don't, sweetheart, but we have to get

you all clean and tidy before his sisters come in. You don't want to frighten them, do you?"

Sometime later, Jo sat nursing Richie as Carrie and Jo's daughters arrived.

"Oh Ma, he came. The baby is here. What's his name?" Nancy asked.

"Richard, but we can call him Richie."

"Hello Richie. I'm your big sister. I will look after you when you are all grown up," Lena promised.

"No, you won't. I will. I am the oldest," Nancy protested.

"Now girls, your ma doesn't need this today. She's tired, and your brother is hungry," Della said to her grandchildren. The twins looked from their gran to their ma and then back to the baby.

"That's all babies do. Eat and poop. Come on, let's go outside and see if Scamp wants to play," Nancy told Lena.

The girls ran off, leaving the adults laughing behind them.

"Pa had the best idea when he got them that puppy. It sure helped them after..." Jo couldn't finish the sentence. Her tears kept falling.

"It did, darling. Now why don't Carrie and I take little Richard downstairs and let you sleep?"

Jo gave up the baby reluctantly. She was tired, but

she was also desperate to be near her baby. Her ma was right, though. She needed some rest.

"Thanks, Ma, for everything."

"I love you, Jo. Sleep well, darling."

Jo closed her eyes, but before she fell asleep, she said a quick prayer, thanking God for letting Richie live. She prayed He would bring Sarah home soon to meet her little brother/cousin.

CHAPTER 28

Sarah nursed Bear as best she could. He slid in and out of consciousness as the hours passed. She racked her brain for everything she had seen Jo do for illness over the years. Bear regained consciousness long enough to tell her what she needed to make the salve. He warned her not to go outside, that it wasn't safe. Sarah promised she wouldn't go, but crossed her fingers as she said it. She wasn't a child. She knew the risks, but she also knew she had no chance of making it home without this man's help. She would wait until he was sleeping before she would go look for them. But when he fell unconscious again and seemed to be developing a fever, she decided she had no choice. She needed to keep him alive. She kept telling herself it was because she needed his protection. She refused to consider there may be another reason. A better one.

She walked quickly and as quietly as she could, carrying Bear's knife with her and telling herself she could throw it just like she had thrown the stones. She found most of what she was looking for and got to refill the water holder, too. She also found a couple of berries which would help assuage the hunger.

She was back in the cave without Bear realizing she had gone. Tala whimpered and wagged his tail. He seemed to be improving daily, too, which was a miracle considering his injuries. She moved toward him to give him a cuddle before she checked on Bear. He appeared to be sleeping and his fever hadn't worsened. Working with the herbs she had gathered, she prepared some bark tea and a salve.

She applied the salve as gently as she could, but her ministrations woke him.

"What are you doing?"

"I made a salve for your injury. I thought it would help it heal."

He frowned, turning to look at her. "You left the cave."

She didn't respond. It was pointless trying to lie when the evidence was all over her hands. She remained silent, working the preparation into his skin.

"I also made you some willow bark tea. It should help with the pain."

"Thank you, Sarah."

She looked up as he said her name. Their eyes met and in that moment, she forgot everything but him. She couldn't tear away her gaze even when he moved slightly forward, as if he meant to kiss her. But he stopped abruptly. "How's Tala?" he asked, his tone tense.

Hurt, and more than a little confused, she answered just as tersely. "He's getting better."

Tala barked and wagged his tail as if to confirm what she said, his gaze moving between them.

Bear tried to get up.

"What are you doing?" she asked.

"We need food. I must go and get some."

"You can't go anywhere. Tell me what to get and I will go." He was going to tell her not to go again. She could tell from the stubborn set of his chin. "Listen to me Bear. I need you to get better quickly so we can both get out of this cave. To do that, you must eat. So please tell me what to get or otherwise we'll all be at risk of food poisoning. I would go and gather everything that looks edible. I could poison the both of us."

Bear laughed, but then immediately winced at the pain his movement caused.

"You are the most stubborn woman I have met."

"You should meet my grandma, Della Thompson. Or Jo. Or Eva. But Becky, she is probably the worst."

"I have heard of these women. Walking Tall is very fond of them. Especially Becky. She is married to He Who Runs. Yes,?"

Sarah nodded, sorry now she had brought up Becky. She loved her adoptive aunt but knew out of all of them, Becky was the one who disapproved of Sarah the most. She had heard Becky tell Jo often enough that she was spoiling her and someday Sarah would break her heart. Becky had been right about that.

Brushing at her eye, she returned her focus to their next meal. "So, what do I look for?"

Bear gave her a lesson on what to gather. She took his knife again and promised not to be long. It was getting rather late, so she hurried as she went about her task. She found quite a few things that looked edible, but decided not to taste anything until Bear gave his approval.

Once back inside the cave, she showed him the fruits of her labors. He praised her hard work, but warned her against the brightest berries. "You eat these, your stomach will hurt for a long time."

"Pity I didn't know that before. I would have cooked them for Edwin's dessert." Immediately she regretted trying to make the joke. The smile left Bear's face and his eyes became cold once more. Disappointed, she turned to prepare their food. Why couldn't she keep her mouth shut? Why did she have to mention him?

***

Bear stared at her as she worked. He couldn't really believe how brave the woman beside him was. He had assumed she was selfish to the core, but she had risked her own safety not once, but twice, to look after him. She had nursed him without consideration for her own feelings. He admired her in so many ways. She was brave, fierce, stubborn, pretty and…white.

CHAPTER 29

The next few days passed without incident. Sarah reheated some of the meat Bear had cooked before he was injured and made it into a soup. She helped Bear eat, then checked his wound. It looked ugly, but it seemed to be healing.

Bear wouldn't let her leave the cave again for fear something would happen to her. So they passed the time telling stories about different people they knew. Bear had some stories about Almanzo and his time in the Indian camp while Sarah told him about Walking Tall and his father and their adventures along the Oregon Trail.

One evening, as they sat at the fire, Sarah finally screwed up the courage to ask him, "Bear, what happened to your back?"

"Nothing." His closed expression warned her not to probe, but she wanted to know more.

"Please tell me. You already know so much about me."

Bear looked at her and then into the flames. He told her how his mother, an Indian maiden, had fallen in love with a white soldier and her tribe disowned her. They had two children before the white man got married to a white woman who had come to the fort. Sarah noticed he didn't call the white man "father." Nor did he use his name. He simply referred to him as "the white man." Bear went on to tell her of his mother's broken heart and how she drowned, leaving him and his elder sister, Snow Maiden, alone. They had lived happily on the outskirts of the soldier's camp for some time. He made her laugh, telling her stories of his sister, who sounded like a lovely woman. He clearly loved her a lot.

"Where is she now? With Walking Tall and his tribe?"

She almost cried at the look of pain on his face as he turned to stare at her.

"She is dead. Her and her child. At the hands of a man like Morgan."

"Oh Bear, I am so sorry."

"He was a scout for the soldiers. He hated them,

but his own people wouldn't accept him either. Like me, he had a foot in both camps. Only his mother had been white. She had been a hostage and, when rescued, was found to be pregnant."

Sarah swallowed hard. She could only imagine what the poor woman had been through. Nobody would care that she had more than likely been raped.

"The poor woman."

Bear didn't appear to hear her. "John Redskin was his name. Not his real name, but that is what they called him. His mother died, he grew up in the camp alone. He started scouting at an early age. Maybe his experiences turned his heart to stone."

"How did your sister fall in love with such a man?"

Sarah immediately regretted asking as Bear responded, "The same way as you fell for Morgan. She couldn't see the real man. He fooled her."

Sarah bit her lip. She couldn't really protest. Edwin Morgan did have her fooled. Or had she just been desperate to prove to her family she could make her own decisions? She didn't want to think about the answer.

"Did he ever love her?"

"I do not think he was capable. But at first, they seemed happy. He was away a lot. She used to sing and laugh all the time. Then he came back. He drank.

Sometimes he was nice, but mostly he was mean. He was convinced Snow Maiden would leave him, too."

"Oh, the poor girl."

"She had a chance to leave, but she wouldn't go. A white man fell in love with her. He would have taken her away to safety. But she said she could not break her promise to John. Even after he beat her, kicked her, and did other horrible things. Still, she would not leave."

"You tried to protect her?"

"Yes. But it was useless. I was too weak, too small. One night he was beating her, and I stood in his way. He used his belt on my back. She tried to fight him off, but he shoved her away. She fell and hit her head on something. I didn't know she was dead until the next morning. Walking Tall had visited the fort, I do not know why. Then John picked a fight with one of his braves. Walking Tall tried to stop it from becoming serious, as that could land all Indians in trouble with the soldiers. He took John home and then found me and Snow Maiden. He killed John, buried Snow Maiden and her child, and took me back to his tribe. I have been there since."

"Oh Bear, what a horrible story. I am so sorry for you and your sister and the baby. Why is life so cruel?"

"There are bad people. White or Indian."

"That is why you said you owe Walking Tall a debt."

"Yes, he saved my life. He would have saved Snow Maiden if he could. As it was, he gave her an honorable burial. She is with my mother now. She is happy."

Sarah hoped that was true, but she wasn't sure if she believed it. She had never given much thought to what happened when a person died. They just weren't there anymore. She cried as she thought of Bear's sister and her baby, which led her to thoughts of her own ma and baby brother.

"My pa ran off on us, too. That's why my ma was on her own on the Oregon Trail. She was hoping to find my pa and settle down on a farm. She and my baby brother died of fever. My older brother died too. It was only me and my sister Carrie left. Rick, my uncle, was going to have us adopted, but then he married Jo, and they became my parents."

"You are lucky you had family."

Sarah couldn't argue with that. But she had never seen how lucky she was. She had thrown their love back in their faces.

"I was such a fool."

"What?" Bear asked.

"Nothing. I'm tired. I think I will sleep now. Thank you for sharing your story with me."

"Goodnight, Sarah."

She lay down on the furs and tried to sleep. She closed her eyes, but her brain wouldn't shut down.

Bear had nobody to protect him when he was younger, whereas she had lots of people. She had been too selfish to see it. If only she could turn back time and tell her family how grateful she was. How sorry she was and how much she loved them. But that wasn't possible.

CHAPTER 30

Bear sat at the fire for some time after Sarah lay down. He hadn't spoken of Snow Maiden for years. The pain of loss was still there, but it was not as agonizing as before. He believed she was with their mother in the spirit world.

He wondered what Sarah had been thinking by the end of their conversation. Several emotions had played over her face—sorrow, pity, understanding, and…something that looked like guilt. Had she realized how lucky she had been to have a family who loved her and protected her? He wondered if this was why the Great Spirit had sent Morgan to meet Sarah. Was it his plan to show her what a wonderful life she had given up? Bear closed his eyes as a wave of pain hit his body. He needed to lie down and get more rest.

He wouldn't be able to protect himself or Sarah if the wound on his shoulder didn't continue to heal.

Bear woke up sometime in the middle of the night. He'd heard something but wasn't sure whether it was an animal or human. Tala had heard it too. He tickled the dog's ears, acknowledging his warning but trying to tell him to be quiet. He didn't want to wake Sarah. He made his way slowly but painfully to the front of the cave. Looking out, he couldn't see anything, but his senses told him they weren't alone. He kept still, only his eyes moving, and finally he saw it. A lit cigarette. Someone was out there. He didn't know if it was a party looking for them or just a random traveler. He moved slowly back into the cave and shook Sarah awake, keeping his hand over her mouth to stop her from making a sound.

"We have company."

Sarah's eyes widened as she stared over his shoulder.

"Do not make a sound."

She nodded, and he took his hand away. She moved quickly to her feet as if to go outside the cave. Instinctively, he put out his arm to stop her. The pain caused a wave of blackness, which almost floored him. She must have sensed it, as she put her arm around him and helped him back to the furs he had lain on.

"We need to put out the fire. Can you do that?"

She nodded.

He watched as she covered the fire slowly with dirt rather than using water. He was impressed. She had been listening when he had explained various tricks to remaining on the run without being seen.

She looked at the cave entrance a few times but made no move to go outside. Instead, once the fire was covered, she picked up Tala and, putting him on her lap, she sat so close to Bear, her shoulder touching his.

He put his good arm around her and drew her close.

"We will be fine. The cave is well protected. They should pass on without seeing us." He hoped she believed him, although he wasn't at all confident in what he was saying. If it was a random stranger, they stood a good chance, but if it was someone tracking them, they were in big trouble.

CHAPTER 31

They sat in silence for what seemed like days, but it was barely more than a couple of hours from when he had seen the light of the cigarette. Tala whimpered a couple of times, but Sarah cuddled him close. Bear kept his ears open, trying to sense whether the stranger was coming closer. Finally, they heard voices. Bear motioned to Sarah to get him his knife, which had been sitting on the rocks near the fire. She reached for it and handed it to him without a word. He winked at her, trying to reassure her everything would be fine. His mind raced at how he could protect her. There were at least two of them out there. Why were they looking in the caves if not searching for them?

He felt Sarah tense beside him at the same time as

he recognized the voice. Morgan. Tala growled before Sarah covered the dog's mouth with her hand.

"Did you hear that?" Morgan asked his companion, their voices carrying into the cave.

"I didn't hear nuthin'. You're real jumpy, Morgan. What's eatin' ya?"

"Shut up, Dyer. I know I heard something. Where's Billy and Jack?" Morgan's voice carried into the cave.

"They headed out earlier than we did. Where did you tell them to meet?"

"Baker City. That should be far enough. Nobody knows any of us there."

"Morgan, you sure nobody saw you with Faulkner's stuff?"

"What do you think I am? Of course, nobody saw me. They were too busy speculating about what happened to him. They were too dumb to think about what he had stacked away in that safe. Only that whore knew and she ain't talking to no-one."

He heard Sarah's intake of breath and only hoped it was not magnified in the cave. He squeezed her closer, willing her not to give them away.

"Tim, I think we got company," Morgan said. "Go into that cave and check."

"You go and check. I didn't hear nuthin'. Could be bears or lions or snakes in there. I ain't movin'."

"Are you yeller?" Morgan taunted.

Bear pulled Sarah closer. He didn't think the argument would end well. What if Morgan was hurt? Would she care?

"Who you callin' yeller? You chicken livered son of a bi—"

The gunshot bit off the end of the sentence as Tim howled in pain. There was another shot and then silence. Bear could feel Sarah shaking, but whether it was with fear or distress, he didn't know. He hoped that Morgan would continue on his way to meet his other friends. He didn't want the man hanging around. If he had to kill him, he would, but then what would Sarah think? She had loved Morgan once. Loved him enough to leave her family and friends behind. That type of love didn't just die, did it?

He closed his eyes. What would he know? He had never paid much attention to women. The ones at camp were forbidden, but none of them had intrigued him. Not like Sarah. She kept his brain and body occupied from morning till night. When she was near him, he wanted to gather her close and kiss her. Her smell tantalized his senses. She made him laugh when he wasn't furious with her. She had a way of looking at him that made his blood boil with frustration. He wondered if she felt anything for him. Her attitude toward him was like that of a friend, but sometimes he caught her looking at him with a wistful expression on her face. But it never lasted.

Now, with her head buried in his arms, it felt so good. So right. As if they were destined to be together. He realized his injury must have done something to his blood. How could a white woman and a half Indian be meant to be together? Theirs was not the type of love affair written about in the stars. He had never heard the elder women tell their children of grand love affairs between white women and Indian braves. It was not accepted by either culture. Neither his nor hers would welcome them or any children they might have with welcome arms. But why was he thinking about children when he hadn't even bedded her?

CHAPTER 32

She sensed him stiffen beside her. It made her wary. She knew he had tried to play down the danger a little. It was his way of protecting her, but she wasn't a child. Or an innocent. Morgan being this close would only lead to trouble. He didn't want her; she knew that now. He never had. He just wanted to bed her and maybe use her to get back at Almanzo and Rick for perceived insults to the Morgan family. It wasn't love, but a deranged sort of lust. How could she have been so stupid not to see him for the villain he was? Bear had shown her more consideration and kindness in the short time she had known him than Edwin had ever done.

She had never felt as safe as she did when in Bear's arms. He had a way of making her feel protected. He had shown he cared about her well-being in the way he had nursed her after she lost the baby, but even before that, too. When she was living in the village, he had brought her food. He had watched out for her the night Edwin had beaten her up, and he was there to protect her when Faulkner wanted to hurt her. He was like her guardian angel. But he only did it out of loyalty to Walking Tall. He wasn't interested in her as a person. As a woman. Yet, he sometimes looked at her the way a man would look at a woman. Or maybe she was imagining it. He didn't have a good opinion of her, so how could he be interested in her in that way? She caught herself. What was she doing thinking like that? There was no future for a couple such as them. Not even her parents, who were good people and accepted everyone for who they were, not the color of their skin, would appreciate Sarah taking up with an Indian.

"Sarah."

She looked up, startled at his whisper. She had been miles away. He looked at her, concern written all over his face. "Are you alright? I don't think it was Morgan who got shot."

He thought she was worried about Edwin? How could he believe she felt anything for him anymore? She hurried to correct him, but before she could get a chance, they heard another gunshot, and another, and then a horrific scream accompanied by an animal's growl.

Tala was desperate to get away from Sarah, but she held onto him tightly. Whatever was out there would hurt all of them.

Bear dragged her down and pushed her head into his chest as he tried to cover her ears. Edwin's screams echoed in her ears. She cried, not because it was him, but because nobody deserved to be in that much pain. Then, mercifully, the screams stopped.

She stayed where she was, not wanting to face the reality of what had probably happened. Here in Bear's arms, she was safe. She closed her eyes until her heart stopped beating so frantically.

"Do you think it's gone?"

Bear grunted. She looked up at him to see his eyes tense with pain. She had been lying on his bad shoulder.

She jumped up. "I am so sorry. You should have said something. What can I do?"

He pulled her back, closer to the other shoulder this time. "You did nothing. It is not your fault."

She sat near him but tried not to lean against him. He didn't look too well. She pushed the hair back from his face, saw the sheen of sweat on his forehead.

"I need to get you some water."

"No, Sarah, you cannot go outside. It is not safe."

"I have to. I won't let you suffer like this."

"There is some water in the can. Later, I will get some more. Promise me you will not leave the cave."

She crawled over to the can and brought it back to him. He refused to drink until she took some. Then he put the can down and pulled her down beside him. Shuddering, she thought about what must have been a wild animal that had attacked Morgan. But with determination, she pushed that fear from her mind. Bear needed her. And she needed him.

CHAPTER 33

Bear held her as she shivered, forcing all thoughts of his pain out of his head. He may have disliked Morgan intensely, but he wouldn't have wished this kind of death on anyone. He wondered if the man had mortally injured the other cat and hoped he had. He didn't have the strength to fight off another wild animal. Sarah moved closer to him, her body almost lying on his. Now he had another problem to worry about, other than the pain. Her nearness was having an effect on his body. He didn't want her to become afraid or uncomfortable. He thought of all sorts of things to distract himself. The woman in his arms was mourning the loss of her man, and he was behaving like an animal.

Sarah looked up at him at that moment. The

expression in her eyes made him blink and blink again. He stilled, not wanting to even breathe. He stared at her, waiting for her to do something.

Sarah's breath caught in her throat as she caught the expression of tenderness in his gaze. Instinctively, she reached up and placed her mouth against his, sensing it was what they both wanted, but sure he wouldn't make the first move. His body went rigid, and for a second she thought she had misread the signals, but then his arms moved around her, pulling her closer. They kissed tenderly for a moment before he pulled away.

"You are a beautiful and amazing woman, but now is not the time for us. Sleep, my tiger." He closed his eyes so she wouldn't argue with him. He hated giving up the opportunity, but he knew this was the wrong time. She put her head against his chest and melded her body as close to his side as possible. There they lay until her breathing told him she was asleep. He had to get outside before she woke up to make sure it was safe. God only knew what the scene looked like, and he didn't want Sarah hurt any more than she had been. But he knew he wasn't in a fit condition to do anything about it tonight.

"Tala, keep guard."

The dog barked as if he understood. Bear smiled as

he cuddled the woman, who had captured his heart closer. It wouldn't last, but for now, he was going to enjoy the feel of her in his arms.

Sarah woke to find herself alone, covered in furs. Where was Bear? She looked around, noticing Tala was missing too. Rubbing her eyes, she got to her feet warily. They must have gone outside. But why? Tala, although improving, wasn't able to defend himself and definitely wasn't up to protecting Bear. The man had regained some of his strength, but it would take time for him to recover properly.

She made her way slowly to the front of the cave, her stomach churning at what she might see. Edwin's screams came back to her, and she dreaded seeing his body, but as she walked out into the light, covering her eyes against the sun's glare, she didn't see anything. She was tempted to call for Bear, but that would put them both at risk if anyone was around. Instead, she decided she had to wait patiently in silence. She sat trying to enjoy the warmth of the sun, but in reality, her heart was beating faster than ever. Where was he? Was he hurt? Would Tala come to get her if he was? Maybe Tala was…

Barking interrupted her thoughts as Tala came bounding through the bushes and into her arms. The dog licked her face in welcome. She ruffled his fur before asking him where Bear was.

CHAPTER 34

Sarah put her hand up to shade her eyes to see if Bear was coming, but there didn't appear to be anyone. Yet Tala wasn't upset; the dog was playfully nipping at her toes. She continued to pet him, wondering at herself. Not only was she sitting outside a cave waiting for an Indian to come home, but she was also playing with a dog. If Almanzo could see her now, he would be struck dumb. She had never shown much interest in animals.

Bear had shown her how men should treat a woman. He had been nothing but kind and protective, never taking advantage of her. Even last night, when she was scared and kissed him, he had held back. He had behaved like a perfect gentleman, whereas she had behaved like a harlot. Her cheeks glowed as she thought of how forward she'd been. She had kissed him, not even waiting for him to make the first move. She had enjoyed it, too. He had been gentle and tender, not demanding like Edwin. He had kept his hands on her shoulders instead of pawing at her. She'd wanted him to do more than he did, and even thinking that thought scared her.

Bear came from a totally different life than hers. He would never be able to live in Portland, not happily anyway. So they didn't have a future together. The thought of never seeing Bear again, never having him hold her, was too much to contemplate. She cried, even as Tala licked the tears from her face. Her distress was so overwhelming that she didn't see or hear Bear return until he called her name. Softly. His expression was full of concern for her.

"Sarah, what is it? Is it…"

"I was thinking about when you take me home. I will never…"

"You still don't want to go home? But I have to take you. I have to pay off my debt to Walking Tall."

"Is that all I am to you? A way to repay your debts?"

He didn't answer, but his expression turned stony.

"Last night, I thought you cared," she ventured. "Did I get that wrong as well?"

Silence.

"I'm talking to you, darn it. The least you can do is respond."

Bear sat down, putting two guns at her feet. She eyed them for a second before looking at him. He shrugged his shoulders.

"What do you want me to say?"

"Something. Anything."

"Sarah, you know there is no hope of anything between us. You will go back to your family. I will…"

"So you don't care."

"Please do not talk for me."

"So you do?"

"Sarah, stop behaving like a child. It doesn't matter how I feel. I will never be allowed to live with a white woman. Can't you see? If we tried to do that in any village, you know, they would hang me from a tree. You would be an outcast. Our children…"

Sarah's heart sang. He did have feelings for her. He had thought about their children. She moved so quickly, she almost caught him off guard as she threw herself into his arms.

"I don't care about any of that. I want to stay with you. I'm never going home."

He held her at arm's length. "You must. You owe it to your parents. And to yourself."

"I am a grown woman. I can make my own decisions. I'm staying with you."

"And still you behave with a selfish heart. I thought you had changed, but you disappoint me." He pushed her away, not roughly, but moving out of her reach. "We must leave here. Morgan's friends may come looking for him."

"Can't we at least talk?"

"What is there to say? You still think you can make decisions without considering other people."

He walked away, leaving her staring after him. What had she done? She had tried to show him she didn't care what people thought, that she would live with him. But instead of making him happy, she had angered him.

CHAPTER 35

*B*ear walked slowly back to the cave, his anger mounting. How dare she make decisions about him and his future? He had a debt to pay to Walking Tall, and after that he intended on…what? What was he going to do?

Before he met Sarah, he had considered tracing his mother's people and taking revenge on them for how they had treated her. But now his heart was no longer full of anger. He didn't care about his mother's people. All he cared about was Sarah. But even thinking about her irritated him. She couldn't just decide she was going to live with him without even considering her family or his obligation to Walking Tall.

Couldn't she see that any relationship between them was out of the question? First, she had a duty to go back and see her family, her parents. Then she had to grieve for all she had lost over the months she had been gone. She wasn't in any fit state to decide her future, let alone his. She was behaving like a spoiled brat, just like she had when she'd run off with Morgan.

He packed up in silence. Sarah stamped around the cave, but he refused to look at her. When he was ready to go, he suggested she take one gun and some water with them.

"Why only one gun?" she asked.

"You know how to shoot?"

She nodded.

"Good, because I do not."

She gave him a look of disbelief, but he didn't bother to explain that most Indians had never fired a rifle.

"It is a long walk, unless we are lucky and find some horses."

"Where are we going, or is that too selfish to ask?"

He glared at her, but she simply glared back.

"We are going to Walking Tall. I told you that before."

They walked in silence along the trail. He kept a lookout for other people, but it seemed they were alone. For that, he was grateful, as Sarah was making as much noise as possible.

"Are you trying to get us caught?"

"Oh, it speaks," she said.

"What do you mean?"

"You haven't said a word to me for hours. Didn't you ever think you may have misunderstood what I was trying to say back there?"

Bear glared at her, wishing she would be quiet and forget about what had been said.

"Well?" she asked.

"I think you made it clear."

"I obviously didn't. I know it's usually the man who starts the conversation, but I didn't think you would. I know…I mean, I hope you have some feelings for me. I know I care about you. Why can't we find a way to be together?"

"It is not possible."

"But why?"

"Sarah, it cannot work."

"Why not? Are you just scared?"

"I am not," he protested, but it was a lie. "At least not for me."

"Well, I'm not scared either," she said. "I don't care what people think."

"That is obvious." He cringed at the look of pain in her eyes, but he didn't make any effort to apologize. It was better she hated him than for her to think they had a future together.

"We will stop here tonight. You light the fire, and I

will go find some fish from the stream." He walked away without looking at her.

"Yes, master."

He ignored her sarcasm and continued walking toward the stream. He had to admire her spirit. It was probably true that she wasn't scared, but she had never lived the life between the middle of two worlds before. It was not a place he was willing to go again. He was never having a family. He would not subject his children to the horrors he had faced as a child. He sat, trying to catch fish, but they obviously sensed his mood. He didn't hear anything until the click of the gun pointed at his head. He turned slowly, kicking himself for letting his guard down so far that a white man had managed to sneak up on him.

"Well, well, what do we have here?"

Bear didn't answer. He had seen that look on a white man's face before. He knew what it meant, and it wasn't pretty.

CHAPTER 36

The Sunday morning service was packed. People who hadn't attended church for years seemed to find the need for solace. The declaration of war had shaken everyone to the core. The younger men seemed eager to go and fight, but the older men and women were less sure. The women didn't want their sons and husbands getting killed or injured. Nobody seemed to believe it would end quickly. Tilly closed her eyes to the gossip and tried to concentrate on what the priest said during his sermon. He had prayed for lasting peace, not just between the States, but for all the people of America.

"Tilly, stop worrying. It will all be fine."

"I hope and pray you are right, Fiona, but I can't help thinking this is going to change a lot of people's lives. I know it is wrong to keep people in slavery, but that isn't the reason why they are fighting, is it? It's a lot more complicated than that."

"I don't understand it either. I just hope nobody we love has to go and fight. If they do, I hope they come back safe. That's all I can do."

Tilly didn't argue. What was the point? She didn't know what was going to happen. She knew if Almanzo went, he would sign up in another state so he wouldn't risk having to fight his Indian friends. She looked at the people filing out of church. Already there were some in the community who held very prejudiced viewpoints. Would the war bring the community together or push it further apart?

"Come on, Tilly, we are all going out to Jo's to meet little Richie. Della is cooking dinner and I'm starving."

Tilly smiled at her husband. Trust him to be thinking about food at a time like this. Still, he was right. They didn't know anything yet, so what was the point of worrying? In the meantime, they had plenty to rejoice about. Jo had delivered a healthy baby, and both were doing well. The whole family would be gathered together again to celebrate the birth. She had to savor these occasions. The memories would help them all get through the war if it came to Portland.

OREGON DISASTER

Later, Jo looked up at her family around her. Richie was a wonderful baby, good from the start. She had recovered from the birth very quickly. Her daughters loved their younger brother, as did Carrie and Bridget. Jo found herself feeling a little less pain when she thought about Rick. She still missed him desperately and wished he were there to share her joy, but having Richie meant she still had a little part of him. Her family was happy. Tilly and Almanzo were obviously well-matched and very happy in their marriage. Carrie was doing well in her studies, and the twins seemed to have settled down as well. Her ma and pa enjoyed good health, as did both her sisters and their families. The only blot on the horizon was Sarah. There was still no word of Rick's niece, the girl she loved like a daughter.

Bridget had told her that David had sent out some telegrams to other newspaper editors in the hope that someone would recognize Sarah, but there had been nothing. Maybe he would have some news today. He and Eva had yet to arrive.

Tilly and Almanzo greeted David as he drew up his wagon and jumped out. He helped his wife down as the boys scrambled out of the back and went off to play with their cousins.

"How are you?" Tilly asked, her smile fading at the look on David's face. Instead, she inched closer to her husband. Something was wrong. She didn't want bad news. Not today.

"Fine. How is Jo?"

"She is inside, tired but happy. Why? Do you have some news?"

David's facial expression was grim. Tilly took a closer look at Eva and realized she had been crying but was now trying her best not to. She went over and put her arms around Eva, drawing her into a hug, her heart beating fast as she wondered what was wrong. Was David leaving already?

"I heard back from one of my newspaper contacts. I think I found Sarah."

"What do you mean 'you think'?" Almanzo asked, clearly worried.

"I kind of hope I didn't."

Tilly stared at David, but Almanzo glared at him.

"What on earth is that supposed to mean?" Almanzo's question was almost accusatory.

"Almanzo, let David explain," Tilly said gently.

"A girl matching Sarah's description is wanted for questioning in a mining town called Tyrell's Pit, over the murder of a man by the name of Faulkner."

Almanzo turned white. Tilly reached for his hand.

"What? When? Sarah wouldn't kill anyone."

"Stop looking at me that way. I don't believe she killed anyone, but I do think it's her. The man is dead, and Morgan and Sarah are now missing and believed to be on the run."

"Edwin Morgan, I wish I had put a bullet in him when I had the chance," Almanzo swore under his breath.

"Then you would be swinging at the end of a rope. Now, do you want to tell Jo? Or should we wait until we have more news?" David asked.

Almanzo looked from David to Tilly and back again. Eva spoke, her voice soft. "I don't think we should say anything. We don't know if it is true. Jo is so happy now. For the first time in a long time. Why tell her before we know for sure?"

"Because she considers Sarah her daughter and has a right to know." Almanzo's tone made Tilly's heart turn over. She could tell her husband was terrified for Sarah.

"I think Eva is right. Can you check if the information is correct?" Tilly asked David. "Maybe it's a coincidence, Sarah and Edwin leaving town around the same time as the man was killed. It could be unrelated." Tilly knew she was clutching at straws and, judging by the look on the others' faces, they thought the same.

"I have a friend over near Baker City. He would go to Tyrell's Pit if I asked him to," David said, but he didn't seem too keen on that solution.

"No, I will go," Almanzo said. "We don't want anyone outside the family knowing this yet. Particularly not the Morgans. God only knows what they would do."

"But why do they suspect Sarah and not Edwin? Surely he is the obvious suspect?" Tilly asked.

"That is what I intend to find out. Tilly, we need to leave now. I want to get going tonight. David, where exactly is this mining village?"

"You can't go alone. You don't know what's waiting for you there," David said.

"I can protect myself."

Tilly kept her mouth shut. She didn't want her husband going alone, but if she said anything, it would look like she thought he was weak.

"Darn it, Almanzo, I didn't suggest you couldn't. But you might want to ask Scott to go with you. He is a better shot than I am. He is also good at tracking."

"Listen to him, darling, please. I don't want you out chasing after Sarah alone. You need help to find her. She could be anywhere." Tilly tried to keep her voice steady. Her husband didn't need her falling apart now. She had to be strong for his sake.

"You win. I will ask Scott. He is up at the house with Becky. Tilly, can you find him and ask him to come to our house, please? I want to get some things done before I ride out. I need to tell the men what I want done over the next few days."

Tilly gave Eva a quick hug, kissed Almanzo on the cheek, and headed toward the house. She had to find Scott and let him know without alerting any other member of the family. That wouldn't be easy.

CHAPTER 37

"I asked you a question."

Still, Bear didn't answer. Instead, he estimated his chances of taking the man down before he shot him. If his shoulder weren't injured, he would have stood a fair chance, but now...

"Get up, nice and slowly. Are there more of you, or are you alone?"

Bear didn't answer. He only hoped Sarah had heard the man and was now hiding. He didn't think her chances of being well-treated were any higher than his.

"I said get up."

The man kicked out, which was his mistake. Bear lunged for his leg and pulled it fast. The man fell to his knees just as the gun went off. The shot went wide, but it was enough to bring the man's friends running.

Bear ducked behind the first man, using his body as a shield. It only worked for a second before the man got his second wind and elbowed him in the stomach while at the same time hitting his injured shoulder. Bear howled with a combination of pain and rage. The second man shot again, this time the shot ricocheted off a rock near Bear's foot.

"Next time, I won't miss. What do you want to do with him, Ernie?"

"I reckon we could have some fun. Tie him to that tree for a start."

"I haven't done anything," Bear said, earning himself a kick from the first man.

"I knew you savages spoke English. We don't care. One less of you is all we care about, that right, Stan?"

Stan spat a wad of tobacco and brown juice out of the side of his mouth, leaving his whiskers covered. From the state of his clothes, it looked like it was a long-standing habit.

Bear spotted Sarah moving behind the men but didn't let on to them in case they saw her, too. He wanted to yell at her to stay away, but he couldn't. God only knew what these men would do to a woman. He had to keep them talking so they wouldn't turn around. He had no idea what she was planning. Why didn't she run now when she had a chance?

A shot rang out, and the man called Stan fell over,

a bullet hole in his head. The look of surprise on his face would have been amusing in other circumstances. Ernie swung around just in time to catch sight of Sarah. He fired his gun, but his aim was off. In response, Sarah fired hers and put a bullet in his leg.

Bear threw himself at Ernie and got his gun away from him.

"You shot me, you stupid woman. Why didn't you shoot the Indian?"

"Cause he didn't mean anybody any harm. The same couldn't be said for you and your friend, now could it?"

"Darn woman. You're white, or have you forgotten?"

"Do you want another bullet?"

"You wouldn't dare."

Her response had the man hopping as the bullet very nearly hit his other foot.

"There is nothing wrong with my aim. I had a brother who taught me well."

"Aw, come on, Miss, you wouldn't shoot an unarmed man now, would ye?" Ernie started pleading for his life, but at a look from Sarah, he shut up quick enough.

"What do you want to do with him?" Sarah asked Bear.

"He is your prisoner, not mine. You decide." Bear walked away, leaving Sarah to come after him.

"What should I do with him?"

"Leave him out here. Shoot him. I do not care either way."

At that, Sarah nearly put a bullet in Bear. How could one man aggravate her so much? She looked at Ernie before throwing the gun quite a distance from him. She filled his water container too and threw that a little nearer.

"You're not going to leave me out here like this, are ye?" Ernie whined.

"Yes."

"But I'll die."

"You might. But I'm guessing you won't. You can crawl to your water bottle and to your gun. By that time, we will be gone."

"This isn't what a God-fearing woman would do."

"Your actions suggest you and God parted ways a long time ago. Maybe your injury will give you time to consider that relationship. I am giving you more than you would have done to him or to me, for that matter," she responded coldly. Then she turned on her heel and walked after Bear. She had to run to catch up with him.

"Were you going to leave me behind?" she asked him.

"I want no part of murder."

"I didn't shoot the other one to kill him. That was an accident. I'm not nearly as good a shot as I claimed to be." She spoke fast, trying to explain herself.

"But you shot at Ernie's foot."

She smirked up at him. "He was lucky I missed."

He stared at her for a second before he burst out laughing. "Why should I be surprised?" He laughed for a little while longer. Then he asked her what she had done with the man.

"I left him his gun and some water. It may take him some time to crawl to them, though."

"You didn't shoot him?"

She stared at him in shock. Surely he knew her well enough to know she wouldn't kill a man if she didn't think she had to.

"You really do have a low opinion of me, don't you? Do you think me a murderer?"

She didn't give him a chance to respond, but marched off ahead of him. She wasn't about to let him see how upset she was. After everything, the fact he would think she would shoot an unarmed man really hurt.

CHAPTER 38

They continued their journey in silence. Bear felt it was wiser not to try to speak to Sarah when she was obviously still upset. She hadn't said a word to him for the whole day and last night had turned in without eating. She had barely said goodnight to Tala, causing the dog to whimper at her feet for a couple of seconds before running back to Bear with his tail between his legs. As the time wore on, Bear felt bad for thinking the worst of Sarah. Had he really believed she was capable of shooting an unarmed man?

Having seen her with Tala and how well she had nursed Bear and the dog back to health, he didn't believe that now. She had a kind heart, she just buried it under a couple of layers. He sensed she had been hurt badly by her pa's betrayal. The fact that her uncle even considered sending her away to an orphanage had obviously left a mark, too. Indians didn't understand an orphanage culture. If a child was left without parents, he or she would be given shelter from a member of the tribe. Usually someone who had lost their own children or whose children had grown up. Bear had heard of orphanages when he grew up at the fort. He had been threatened with it more than once, usually when he had upset John Redskin over something or other. They had been portrayed as scary places. He had never visited one, so he had no idea if it was or not.

He glanced at Sarah when she woke up the next morning. She hadn't slept well. He knew as he had been awake too, but even if he hadn't, the black circles under her eyes would have given her away.

"Breakfast?"

She didn't answer him, so he tried again. She needed to keep her strength up. Today, they would start climbing into the mountains.

"You need to eat."

She took the food without comment and ate it all. Then she rolled up her furs and got ready to move out. He wanted her to talk. He didn't care what she spoke about. He missed the sound of her voice.

"I am sorry."

She glanced at him but didn't say a word.

"Sarah."

"I heard you. Let's move out."

"Am I forgiven?"

She looked up at him, the look in her eyes sending a shaft of pain through him. "I can't believe you thought I was capable of that. I know I was horrible to the little boy back at the laundry. I should have helped his ma. I know what you think about me leaving my family. But murder? I didn't mean to kill Faulkner, but he was going to sho — "

Before she could finish, Bear pulled her into his arms and kissed her. Her lips were warm against his. She dropped the fur and wrapped her arms around his neck, pushing her body against his. He pulled her as close as he dared as his lips explored hers. She tasted of mint and something unique. He was the one who broke the kiss.

"I am sorry. You were only trying to defend me. I got angry because you put yourself in danger."

"I had to. You couldn't defend me very well if Ernie had tied you up."

He kissed her again. "You always have an answer for everything. No wonder Walking Tall calls you Miss Sassy."

She tried to pull away, but he wouldn't let her. Instead, he kissed her eyes, her nose, from one ear to the other before returning to her lips. He tried to tell her how he felt without using words.

* * *

Sarah couldn't believe she was in his arms and he was kissing her. She wanted more. She wrapped her arms around his neck and pulled him toward her as he deepened the kiss. Kissing him was totally different from anything she had ever experienced. It was like coming home, but in an exciting way. She never wanted it to stop.

"We need to get moving," he said, breaking their kiss. "We have to cover quite a bit of distance today."

"Maybe I should have shot Ernie after all," she joked. He smiled, making her heart soar. He knew she was only teasing. They were making progress.

She kissed him lightly on the lips once more before helping him to dismantle their small camp. She put the dirt over the fire to make sure it was out while he packed up their meager supplies.

"How far is it to Walking Tall's camp?"

"Not far. It will take us three days if all goes well."

Three days of walking. She would hate to know what he considered far. Yet it was only three days.

After that, they would be surrounded by people who knew them. Whatever chance they had of finding a way to be together would depend on how much progress they made over the next three days. Bear's lack of trust in people, red and white, would make it difficult.

CHAPTER 39

Bear walked in the direction of the camp, his senses on high alert. He didn't want another surprise like the last one. He couldn't remember ever letting someone creep up on him like that. It was Sarah. His feelings for this woman had his head melted more than if he had spent ten days out in the middle of the desert in the big sun. He knew he loved her. He guessed he had loved her from the start, despite not liking how she behaved. It was her bravery and guts, and now, also her kindness and the care she showed for Tala, that had him smitten. Even the fact she hadn't put a bullet in Ernie had lifted her higher in his estimation. And the fire between them was fierce. It threatened to extinguish both of them. He had heard of great passion. He believed it was what his mother and father had before his father had given in to the pressure to marry a white woman. Would Sarah end up feeling that same pressure? If they did become one, would she end up leaving him? He never minded being alone before, but after being with Sarah, he didn't think he could handle it. It was better that they stopped things between them before they reached the point where going back was not an option.

He stared at her, walking slightly ahead of him. How would he live with himself when she went back to her own family? He believed she would. There was no reason not to. Morgan was dead, and with him, all knowledge of the baby she had once carried. She could return as a single woman, one day marry a white man, and have children with him. If he really loved her, that is what he would wish for her.

She turned to look at him, her smile growing a little shaky as he took a couple of seconds to return it. She walked back toward him.

"What's wrong? You're frowning."

"I was just thinking of the weather. It looks like it might rain."

She looked up at the clear blue sky.

"I wish you wouldn't lie to me. You're not very good at it."

He didn't respond. What could he say? She would only argue and tell him he was wrong.

* * *

SARAH WALKED QUICKER, hoping that by doing so, the day would be over sooner. She wanted to light a fire and lie in the firelight with Bear. She wished they would come to a river before they set up camp. She could do with a wash, and she wasn't the only one.

The butterflies in her stomach thrilled at the thought of seeing Bear in the river, the water clinging to the muscles on his chest. She wondered if he thought about her body. He had seen it when he nursed her, but this would be different. She was so busy making plans she didn't notice Bear had stopped and was staring ahead of them. Then she heard what had caught his ear: the sound of hooves.

The riders were approaching fast. She took out the gun, moving back toward Bear.

"Put the gun away, Sarah. It is Walking Tall and his men."

"How do you know?"

"I saw his signal a little while back. I wasn't sure what it meant until now. Put the gun away."

She did what he said, hastily hiding it in the folds of her clothes. She wasn't about to throw it away. She trusted Bear, but what if the visitors weren't friendly? She stood and waited, wishing he would take her hand or put an arm around her. Instead he stood rigid, his face an unreadable mask. Tala ran toward the horses and then decided against it and ran back to Sarah. He stood by her. She ran her hands over his fur, grateful that at least one of her companions definitely loved her.

CHAPTER 40

"Miss Sassy. At last. You have caused us many nights without sleep," Walking Tall said in greeting.

Sarah stared not at Walking Tall, but at Almanzo. She couldn't believe he was there. She stiffened as he got off his horse, expecting him to start yelling at her. Instead, he ran over and whisked her off her feet.

"Thank God you're safe. I was so worried about you. We all were. Sarah, I can't believe it."

Sarah hugged him back and then hugged Scott before Walking Tall also grabbed her into a big bear hug. Now the tears ran down her face. Her family looked more relieved than angry. They hadn't given her a tongue-lashing but had shown how much they cared for her. Relief flowed through her. Then she noticed Bear was hanging back, outside of their little circle. She went to him and, taking his hand, dragged him back to where her family was standing.

"I owe this man my life. Thank you, Walking Tall, for sending Bear to look for me. I wouldn't be here if you hadn't."

Almanzo held his hand out to Bear, as did Scott. "Thank you, Bear. Walking Tall told us he had sent a man out to check on Sarah. We really appreciate everything you did."

"It was nothing," Bear mumbled.

"Come, let us make camp. We have much to talk about," Walking Tall said, giving Almanzo and Scott a look Sarah couldn't interpret. She decided not to question it. The men would have questions for her, and she couldn't wait to find out how Carrie, Rick, and Jo were doing.

They made camp very quickly. Walking Tall cooked while Sarah collected water. She hoped Bear would come to the river with her, but he stayed with Walking Tall and talked. Scott and Almanzo seemed very busy with their horses, but as she didn't want them to give her a talking-to about running off, she left them to it. The meal was eaten in uncomfortable silence until Sarah decided she had had enough.

"Well, you might as well get it off your chest. I admit I was selfish and foolish to run off. Edwin Morgan wasn't as bad as you made him out to be."

Sarah looked at Almanzo, who opened his mouth to respond, but she beat him to it. "He was worse, much worse. But he is gone now, and I have learned my lesson. So, lecture over."

"Is that what you think we were going to do? Give you a talking-to? You haven't changed that much then, Sarah."

Scott's words stung. Sarah looked from one to the other, but they wouldn't meet her eyes. She looked at Walking Tall, who stared back at her with pity. Suddenly, she knew they had bad news for her, and nobody knew how to tell her. She bit back her fear. "What happened?"

Almanzo looked shocked, as did Scott, but Walking Tall just kept staring. This time, the pity in his eyes was accompanied by admiration.

"Sarah, after you left, we had some trouble and…" Almanzo started.

"Spit it out," she pushed.

"Rick died. There was an attack, and he was trying to save his family. Everyone else survived, but he was killed."

Sarah stared at Almanzo. She could see his mouth opening and closing, but she couldn't hear what he was saying. Rick was dead. She was too late. She couldn't tell him how sorry she was. How much he'd meant to her. How she didn't mean to hurt him.

"No, it can't be," she cried. "Not Rick. He was too young. What about Jo? Carrie, the girls?" She rocked back and forth as she berated herself loudly for being so selfish and self-serving. Bear moved quickly to her side and pulled her against his chest, holding her tightly as she sobbed. She cried not just for Rick but for Jo, Carrie, the twins, and herself. Her baby. Everything. Once she started crying, the tears wouldn't stop. The other men said nothing. Silence prevailed, broken only by the sounds of her sobs. When they had subsided, Bear released her slightly, but she still sat with her head against him. She didn't care what anyone thought. She needed him, his strength, and his protection.

"Sarah, Rick loved you just like his own child. He considered you, me, and Carrie as much a part of his family as he did his own girls. Jo too. She worries about you daily. She can't wait for you to meet Richie."

"Who is Richie?" Jo couldn't have a new husband already. She loved Rick. But then she supposed she had found Bear with Edwin gone only a few days previously. But that was different. She had never truly loved Edwin. Now she knew what love was. She recognized her feelings for Edwin had been a mix of attraction and a way to hurt Rick. She wanted her uncle to feel how she had felt upon hearing he was going to send her away. But he hadn't. He had given her a home, his love, and support, and she had thrown it in his face.

"Jo was pregnant when Rick died. She didn't know. Her baby was born about three weeks ago. They are both doing very well, and they're looking forward to meeting you." Almanzo smiled at her; she could see he was being genuine. He did care about her, just like a real brother.

"Sarah, we have other problems."

She turned to stare at Scott. Surely nobody else could be dead?

"It seems you and Edwin are wanted for questioning over the murder of someone called Faulkner."

Before Sarah could answer, Bear spoke.

"It was me. It had nothing to do with Sarah. I killed him."

Shocked, she looked at Bear in disbelief. He was going to give himself up for the crime she had committed. Over her dead body.

"That's a lie. He's trying to protect me, but it was me, not Bear, who killed Faulkner. And I only did it because he was going to shoot Bear. I will swear to that in court."

"You might not get to court. They seem to prefer meting out their own justice in that part of the country. Did you steal his gold, too?"

"Gold? What gold? I didn't want anything of his."

Sarah quickly explained the situation with Edwin, owing money to Faulkner and offering her services to work it off.

"Where on earth was Morgan?" Almanzo asked.

"He had run off with all of my savings the night before." Sarah didn't mention the baby. She glanced at Bear, but he didn't say anything. Maybe it was better kept a secret.

"Then who stole his gold?"

Bear coughed. "That may have happened after he died." Bear explained how they had heard Morgan outside the cave and how he had mentioned a girl, a soiled dove, who would not be able to turn them in.

"A spoiled dove was murdered, too. The sheriff blamed her death on a disgruntled customer."

"So where is Morgan now? We need to bring him in to give evidence," Scott said.

"That may be a problem," Sarah said, her eyes on Bear.

CHAPTER 41

"He is dead. Not by my hand. He was killed by a mountain lion. I buried him and his friend."

Almanzo ran his hands through his hair, a gesture he had always done when he was upset. Sarah put her arm on his shoulder. "I'm sorry I brought all this trouble to your door."

Walking Tall broke his silence. "It seems the death of Mr. Morgan is a good thing. He stole the gold, he murdered the woman and the death of Faulkner is on his hands. He should be the one to pay for the crime."

"He also beat Sarah. The woman at the store in town and at the laundry can tell the lawman that is true," Bear added.

Sarah wanted to hit Bear as she turned crimson under the combined glares of Scott and Almanzo.

"Morgan beat you?" Almanzo's cold tone told her he was struggling to keep his temper.

She nodded, not wanting to say more. She didn't want her brother, or any member of her family, knowing how badly he had treated her. She had some pride. She hoped Bear wouldn't give out any more information.

"He Who Runs, do you agree with me?" Walking Tall asked Scott, using his Indian name. Scott gave Sarah a long look before nodding his head. "When we go home, I will tell David. He will send a telegram to his contacts. I'm sure we can get the sheriff to back us up. We should head back to Portland early tomorrow."

Sarah glanced at Bear but his face was, once more, an unreadable mask.

"I'm not going home," she said, causing all four of the men to stare at her.

"What do you mean, you're not coming home? You're coming if I have to drag you there myself."

"I am a grown woman, Almanzo. I don't have to do what you say."

"But you have to come home. Jo won't rest until she sees you are alright," Almanzo insisted.

"You can tell her I'm safe and that I'm not leaving."

"But you can't stay here, in the middle of nowhere. Do you have any idea how dangerous these woods can be?" Almanzo continued, his tone annoying her.

Putting her hands on her hips, Sarah stared straight at her brother. "You taught me how to defend myself. I threw a rock at Faulkner and at a mountain lion. I shot one man in the head and another in the leg. I think I know how to look after myself just fine."

Walking Tall laughed, causing everyone to glare at him. It didn't deter him.

"I don't see what is so funny," Sarah snarled at the chief.

"You are so like Becky. It makes me laugh. I should apologize, but I will not. You are Miss Sassy."

Sarah pulled herself onto her tippy toes, but before she could answer, Bear spoke.

"Sarah will return with you tomorrow. She knows she needs to go back and apologize to her adopted mother. She also must say sorry to her sisters and those she caused to worry. She is no longer the selfish, self-centered brat who ran away. She has grown much in these past weeks. You will see that by her actions tomorrow."

With that, he walked away, leaving Sarah staring after him. She couldn't go after him, not in front of her brother, uncle and Walking Tall. She would have to speak to him in the morning. She nearly screamed with frustration as Almanzo bedded down on one side of her and Scott on the other. Were they protecting her honor, or making sure she didn't run away again? She punched her furs repeatedly as she tried, but failed, to sleep. She sat up and looked to the other side of the fire where Bear had lain his rug. He seemed to have no issue sleeping.

CHAPTER 42

Bear heard her rustling, twisting, and turning, but he lay as still as a dead mouse. He wished she would fall asleep. It took a long time, but finally, he heard her gentle snores. He rolled silently to his side, packed up his fur, and was about to walk out when he caught Walking Tall staring at him. His Chief indicated with his eyes that he wished to speak to him. Bear walked, knowing Walking Tall would follow. He had to get his thoughts together.

"Why do you fly like a thief in the night?"

Bear stared at Walking Tall, trying to work out what he was being accused of, but the man's face gave nothing away.

"I didn't see the gold and I only killed a mountain cat."

"I know this. So why run away now?"

"I am not running." At the look on his Chief's face, he shrugged his shoulders. "It is difficult."

"You share her feelings?"

Bear nodded. He couldn't say it out loud. He loved her, but it was impossible.

"You have chosen a difficult path," Walking Tall said, looking at him closely.

Bear met his Chief's eyes. "I didn't choose it on purpose."

Walking Tall smiled in response. "The Thompson women, and I include Sarah in that group, as she has learned a lot from Jo, are strong-minded women. They do not seem to know fear. At least they do not let being afraid stop them from following their hearts."

"I am not a coward. If it were only me, I would do anything to stay with Sarah. But what if we have children? They will suffer like I did."

"Not with my people. My people will accept you, her, and them."

Bear stared at his Chief.

"You do not believe this to be true?" Walking Tall asked.

"I think you like to believe it would be this way, but we both know your people do not accept me. Why—"

"Why do you feel this way? What proof have you

that what you are saying is true?" Walking Tall interrupted, his voice harsh.

"Because none of them would let me marry their maidens. They made that obvious."

Walking Tall looked at him, a fierce expression on his face. "My people accepted He Who Runs, and he is 100% white. My people have no problem with someone who holds himself upright with pride. You behave like a wounded Tala, snarling at those who try to be friendly. It is not only Miss Sassy who needs to grow up. You do, too. Not everyone is like John Redskin or your grandparents. You must put your past behind you, or you will never find happiness."

Bear stared at Walking Tall in shock. The Chief was blaming him for the fact he felt like an outsider. He opened his mouth to argue, but he had nothing to say. When he had met Sarah, his heart had been full of hatred toward all those people who had hurt his mother, his sister, and ruined his childhood. But maybe Walking Tall was right? His tribe had not been responsible for anything that had happened to Bear, yet he judged those people with the same view as he had other Indian tribes.

"I see you have many things to consider. I suggest you leave like you planned, but instead of running away, confront your demons. Only then will you find true happiness."

Bear couldn't say anything. He nodded and turned to walk away. Walking Tall came closer and dragged him into a hug. "Take care, my friend. I will see you soon."

CHAPTER 43

Sarah woke late the next morning as the men broke camp. She immediately looked for Bear, but she couldn't find him. Her heart knew he had left. She had sensed he would, which is why she had tried to stay awake.

"Walking Tall, take me with you to your village, please."

"No, Miss Sassy. You need to go home."

"But I want to be with Bear."

"He is not at my village. You need to let him go. You know this. Deep in here."

Walking Tall pointed at Sarah's heart before turning back to his horse. He mounted swiftly.

"Will you ride with me?"

She nodded. Almanzo helped her mount. She put

her arms around Walking Tall and cried freely against his back.

It took two days for them to reach home, by which time Sarah was travel sore and exhausted, but her real pain was the loss of Bear. He obviously didn't love her enough to risk a future with her. Almanzo and Scott tried to engage in conversation, but she kept quiet. Walking Tall didn't say much. He had a way of looking at her, making her feel he knew what she was thinking, but he didn't comment.

"We will be home in an hour. I think we should stop at my home and tidy up a bit," Almanzo suggested.

"Tilly won't want to see me," Sarah muttered, her face going scarlet. She had treated Tilly badly as well, even if the girl didn't know about it. She had said horrible things to Carrie.

"Tilly is just as worried about you as everyone else. She will help you clean up. I do not want Jo to see you looking like this."

She looked down at her blood-stained dress and realized Almanzo was right.

Tilly came running as they rode into her yard. She went straight to Almanzo and hugged him tight. Then she spotted Sarah. Sarah dismounted and stood, unsure of her welcome. Tilly came over and put her arms around her, pulling her close. Almanzo's wife's gesture was nearly the undoing of Sarah. She tried to hold back the sobs but failed.

"Almanzo, get me some water. I'm sure Sarah would like a bath. Scott, do you want to get home or stay for dinner? Walking Tall, you are welcome to join us, of course."

"Walking Tall and I will head up over to David's. We need his help with something. Almanzo, are you coming?"

Almanzo wasn't going to, that was obvious until Tilly practically chased him away.

"Go on. This will take some time and Sarah needs her privacy," Tilly instructed her husband.

Almanzo gave Sarah a long look before getting back on his horse. "Stay here. Do not go to Jo without me."

Sarah bristled at his tone, but she held her tongue. She just stared back at him as he rode out.

"He's been worried about you. When he gets all masterful like that, it's only because he cares," Tilly explained.

* * *

Tilly couldn't believe Sarah was standing in front of her. It was obvious from her clothes she had been through an ordeal. She was very thin and her body showed bruising and other marks. Tilly said nothing, feeling Sarah would talk if she wanted to. Instead, she filled the bath, made Sarah some tea, and found her some clean clothes.

"Thank you Tilly, you are very kind."

"We were all worried about you. I'm glad you're home safe."

"Tilly, I'm sorry I wasn't more welcoming to you. I said some horrible things, too. I hope you can forgive me."

"I didn't hear you say anything," Tilly said.

"I'm glad, but I said them all the same. I just want you to know I am not that girl anymore," Sarah said quietly.

"I would like it if we were friends. Almanzo thinks the world of you."

"I'm not so sure. Your husband wants to slap me right now. He got very annoyed with me out on the trail. I didn't want to come back."

Tilly stared at Sarah. "Why ever not?"

"I wanted to stay with Walking Tall and his tribe."

"But why?"

"I fell in love. For real this time, with the man Walking Tall sent to save me."

"An Indian?"

"He is the finest man I have ever met," Sarah said.

"I'm sure he is," Tilly said. "Almanzo's mother

found happiness with an Indian. It is not an easy path, but it can work for some."

Tilly nearly fell into the bath water as Sarah spontaneously hugged her.

"You understand, thank you. Almanzo thought I was being silly."

"I don't think he would think that because you fell in love with an Indian, Sarah. He probably just wanted you to come home and see Jo before you decided to live somewhere else. Your family is different from most. I don't think they would care who you brought home so long as the man was decent and treated you well."

"Not like Edwin."

"Your family certainly doesn't like him," Tilly said, not wanting to be too hard on the man Sarah had run away with.

"They were right about him. He was horrible, and I was so stupid. I thought I was in love, but I wasn't. I just wanted to prove I wasn't a child anymore. Instead, I showed how selfish and spoiled I really was."

Tilly knew Sarah was speaking the truth, but she wasn't about to crush her when she was obviously distraught. Instead, she tried to reassure her all would be fine. "That is all in the past. You are home now and Jo will be delighted. Carrie too. She really missed you. She was so hurt when you didn't write back to her."

"I never got any letters. I guess we moved around a lot."

Tilly was sure that was an understatement, as she realized Sarah was a lot thinner than she'd first appeared. The marks of abuse were all over her body. The poor girl had been through a horrible time. "Do you want to go and see Jo now?"

"But Almanzo said to wait for him."

"I know he did, but sometimes my husband says things for the wrong reasons. He is trying to protect both of you, but I don't see the point in putting it off. Jo needs to see you. She wants to see you, and I think you need to see her."

"Tilly, thank God Almanzo had the sense to marry you. Thank you."

Tilly linked arms with Sarah and together they walked over to Jo's house.

CHAPTER 44

Jo sat at the window nursing Richie. Feeling restless, she tried to pinpoint the reason for her anxiety. Almanzo had disappeared very quickly the other day. Scott too. It had something to do with Walking Tall. Surely there wasn't more trouble between her neighbors and her Indian friends. She hadn't heard of any and knew Walking Tall's tribe would not be the cause of any dissent. She rocked her baby back and forth.

Looking up, she caught sight of two women walking up the trek to her house. Tilly, she recognized, but the other woman, similar in age to Tilly, was a stranger. Jo looked closer. There was something familiar about the girl.

"Bridget! Carrie! Come quick."

Carrie ran into the room, followed closely by Bridget, both of them white-faced. "What's wrong, Jo? Is it the baby?"

"Carrie, Sarah's outside. She's come home. It is her, isn't it?"

Bridget looked out the window as Carrie ran to the front door. Bridget and Jo stared as the young girl ran toward Tilly and Sarah and almost knocked them down.

"Thank the Lord, Bridget, our little girl is home."

Bridget couldn't answer, tears running down her face.

Sarah came into the room hesitantly. "Jo, I am so sorry. I…"

"Sarah, darling, you're back. Come here and give me a hug. This is Richie, your baby brother."

Jo pulled the girl she considered a daughter closer. She held onto her as if she would never let her go, both her and Sarah in tears. Tilly had her arm around Carrie, who was also crying.

The twins came running in to find out what the noise was all about. They came to a standstill when they saw Sarah.

"Get out. We don't want you here. Go away." It was Nancy who said it, but, judging by Lena's face, she spoke for both the twins.

Jo looked at her daughters in shock. "Stop it, girls. Don't speak to Sarah like that."

"You left us and didn't say a word. You made Ma cry. A lot. We hate you." With that, the girls ran off, leaving Sarah stricken, looking after them.

"Sarah, I'm sorry. They will be punished for their behavior."

"No, Jo, don't. They're right. I did hurt you and Rick. And I'm so sorry. I loved him so much."

"He loved you too, Sarah, and he would be delighted you came home. Bridget, can you bring in some tea? Carrie, can you help her, please?"

Tilly followed Bridget and Carrie, leaving Sarah and Jo alone.

"Sarah, darling, I'm so happy you are home. Please tell me you're here to stay."

Sarah bit her lip, making Jo's stomach heave. She wanted to grab the girl and never let go.

"I promise I will never run away again. That's the best I can do, Jo."

Jo sensed Sarah's story wasn't over yet. She smiled through her tears. "That's good enough for me, darling. Now why don't we take this little man out to the kitchen and see what goodies Bridget has baked?"

Sarah let Jo put her arm around her shoulders. Jo had to bite back a remark about how thin her daughter was. For now, she had to tread lightly. Sarah had been through some horrors, that much was evident, and Jo was going to make sure nothing hurt her daughter again.

Later, Sarah lay in her bedroom. Alone. Carrie had opted to sleep with the twins, who were still upset over Sarah's return. Tilly had gone home to Almanzo. She said she and Almanzo would return tomorrow. Jo had stayed with Sarah for a while, but she didn't ask any questions. She spoke about Rick, how ill he had been, and how bravely he had fought to keep his family safe. Sarah had cried when Jo told her how much Rick loved her and had regretted ever saying he would put the girls into an orphanage. That had simply been said in panic. He would never have been able to abandon them. Sarah didn't tell Jo anything other than that Edwin was dead. Jo accepted she needed time to talk.

"Sarah, darling, you can tell me anything. I won't ask any questions. You do what you feel is right. But remember, I love you and I don't care what you did or didn't do when you were away. You are my daughter, and nothing will ever change how I feel about you."

Sarah knew her adoptive mother spoke the truth. It helped a little. But when she was left alone, she let the tears fall. She wished Bear were with her.

She didn't get to see the other members of the

extended Thompson family until church services that Sunday. She dressed with care, wanting Jo's family to see she had grown up and matured.

"Sarah, they love you too. Everything will be fine."

Sarah smiled at Jo, wishing she shared her confidence. She was dreading meeting the rest of the family, Grandma Della, and Becky in particular. Those two had been the most vocal about how selfish she had been growing up.

She walked into the church, grateful Jo was beside her. The family smiled at her but didn't get to say anything as the priest had started the service. Afterward, they met outside.

"Sarah, we are so pleased to see you back. You look well," Eva said, smiling.

"No, she doesn't, Eva. She looks like skin and bone. No doubt you had a difficult time."

Sarah swallowed hard as she returned Becky's stare, looking her in the eye. "I was wrong to go, but I survived. And I came back."

Becky smiled, the approval lighting up her eyes. She put her arm around Sarah and drew her close. "We are delighted you're home."

Sarah relaxed as Della also hugged her close. Nobody gave her a lecture, and they all seemed genuinely glad to see her. Scott motioned her aside. "Walking Tall said to tell you he is safe."

Sarah nodded, knowing they spoke of Bear. Her heart beat faster and the tears would come, but later. Now she had to keep a smile on her face for her family. She wouldn't do anything else to upset these people who had only ever shown their love and support for her.

A few weeks later, the family found out the charges against Sarah had been dropped. Edwin's body and the gold had been found, and that was evidence enough of his involvement in the murder of the whore. Everyone assumed he had also killed Faulkner. Mrs. Morgan had collapsed when she was told. Some days later, she and her husband closed up their house and returned to the East. Nobody was sorry to see them go.

Sarah gradually rebuilt a relationship with her sister and the twins, Nancy and Lena. The children took a bit longer to come around than the adults, but they eventually seemed to forget their grudge. The fact Sarah spent hours playing with them, dressing their dolls, and allowing them to bandage her as a patient as they played nurse probably helped.

Jo kept her promise and never asked questions. There were times Sarah was almost overwhelmed with the need to tell Jo everything that had happened, but she didn't. She did tell Jo about Bear and how he had saved her from Edwin. From the packet of food that first day to getting away from Tyrell's Pit. She left out the saddest parts. Jo had her own demons to deal with, although, from what Sarah could tell, little Richie was helping her.

Every night, Sarah went to bed wishing she knew where Bear was and how he was feeling. As the weeks passed, she gradually came to accept he didn't share her feelings. He cared for her, but she loved him. She would never love another the way she felt about him. If only her love were enough for the both of them.

CHAPTER 45

Bear looked around the village. Nothing seemed to have changed, yet everything had. Everyone was friendlier to him than they had ever been. The older braves encouraged him to visit them and a couple had hinted they would be open to their daughters moving into his teepee.

"You look happy, my friend."

"Thank you Walking Tall. I feel better."

"You have cleansed your demons?"

"Yes. I found what is left of my mother's tribe. They live on a reservation. My grandparents are dead, but I found an uncle. He told me the story of how my mother left. It seems my beliefs were not the true story."

"It is often the case with childhood memories. Your mother may have told you things to help her live with her actions. She may not have told you everything. You may have remembered it in a different way. It is normal. It happens."

"But I spent so many years hating my mother's people when they would have welcomed me and Snow Maiden. We could have lived with them. We would have been safe." Bear had taken a while to believe his uncle spoke the truth, but finally saw he had no reason to lie.

"But then you would be living on a reservation. Is that what you would want?"

Bear shook his head. He had been filled with sadness at seeing how his mother's people lived. His uncle accepted that the ways of the past had gone. Even when Bear had told him about Walking Tall living free in the mountains, his uncle had warned him that in time, even this tribe would find itself on a reservation somewhere.

"He is right. It may happen. But I will not go to live anywhere the white man tells me. I live in freedom or not at all. That is my choice and the choice of all those who live here."

"How did you know I was thinking about that?" Bear asked Walking Tall, shocked at how easily the man had read his mind.

"It is the obvious question. Why are we not on a reservation? How much longer will we be free?"

Walking Tall looked into the distance. "The war between the white men will last a long time. Maybe three seasons or more. Nothing will be the same once it is over. Maybe we will be allowed to live in peace when they have finished fighting each other. Who knows? For now, we must enjoy our life as it is. Forget the past and the future and enjoy the present."

Bear wished he were as wise as Walking Tall, but he couldn't forget the past. Not the recent past, anyway. Every night when he went to sleep, he dreamed of her. It wasn't just at night either. She was always with him. If he concentrated hard enough, he could feel her skin, smell her hair. She was all around him. He wanted to be with her. He knew she was the one for him. He wasn't interested in marrying anyone else.

"Miss Sassy has returned to full health. Jo and her family welcomed her home."

Again, Walking Tall had read his mind. He looked at his Chief. "Is she happy?"

Walking Tall stared back at him. "About as happy as you are, I would think."

"I want her as my woman. I want children with her. But I cannot ask her to share my life."

"Why not?"

Bear stared at Walking Tall. What could he mean

by that? He, of all people, knew how difficult it would be.

"You want her. She wants you. Everything else will work its own way out. It will not be easy, but at least you may find happiness."

"Can we live with you?"

"Of course, you will always be welcome here. But you may prefer to try living in the white man's world. I do not think Miss Sassy is well suited to living in a teepee. She may prefer a house."

Bear smiled. The chief was probably right. For all Sarah had said about wanting to live with him, the attraction of the Indian lifestyle may wear a bit thin.

"Will you ask her? Jo has invited us to visit her later. Mia, Almanzo's sister, wishes to see him. It is a good time for you to see if Miss Sassy still wants you."

Bear swallowed hard. He hadn't considered the fact Sarah may have changed her mind.

CHAPTER 46

Sarah watched as her whole family filled the room for little Richie's christening. The church service was lovely, but the family gathering at Jo's house was extra special. It was the first time since she had returned that the whole family was together. Although she had seen and spoken to everyone individually, this was different. She looked at her ma. Jo was holding the babe in her arms, smiling, but her eyes were glistening with tears. Sarah held back a sob. She missed her uncle Rick, the best father anyone could have. She would give almost anything to see him one more time, to apologize, and to thank him for taking care of her and Carrie. But that chance would never come. Instead, there was a room full of people whom she owed an apology.

"Before you all go home, I would like to say something, please." Sarah stood, trying to stop her voice from trembling with nerves.

"Oh, don't tell me you are running away again?" Grandma Della asked.

"No, Grandma Della, although if you keep teasing me like that, I just might." Everyone laughed, including Della. Sarah looked around her; she was so lucky to have all these people in her life. She didn't deserve any of them, yet they loved her and had accepted her back into the family.

"I wanted to say thank you to each one of you for your support and help since I came home. Most of all, I wanted to apologize for my thoughtless, selfish actions. I was a child when I left. I don't know how to tell you how sorry I am, but believe me, I have learned my lesson."

"We know you have, Sarah, and you are back here in the middle of your family. This is your home."

Sarah sent a look of thanks to Jo before turning to Tilly and Almanzo. "Tilly, thank you for your friendship. You are the ideal woman for my brother. I know you are very happy together, and I am truly glad. I am sorry the Morgan family made your arrival in town less than welcoming."

Tilly smiled but didn't reply. Almanzo looked as if he was going to speak, but she gave him a look, so he closed his mouth.

"Carrie, you are the best sister anyone could have. If I could take back the months of worry, I would. I will never knowingly hurt you again. Thank you for forgiving me."

Carrie rushed to her side and gave her a hug, leaving her breathless.

Silence reigned. The family seemed to sense she wasn't finished.

"Becky, you were one of my harshest critics, along with Grandma Della." Both women looked uncomfortable. She hurried on, "I wanted you both to know I have seen the error of my ways, and the spoiled little madam you used to know is a thing of the past."

"We know that, darling. You only have to spend five minutes with you to see how much you have matured."

"Thank you, Becky." Sarah gave her aunt a smile before turning her attention to Bridget. "Bridget, I promise never to ignore your advice again. I should have listened to you when you tried to warn me."

"Never could put an old head on your shoulders, sweetheart."

Sarah knew that was true, and if she was honest, she couldn't say she wished she had never left. Then she wouldn't have met Bear. Where was he? Was he happy? Would she ever see him again? A discreet cough from her grandfather was enough to bring her attention back to her family.

"Finally, thank you, Jo. For not only being the best ma anyone could ask for, but for welcoming me back home. You have never once blamed me for what I did. You could have closed the door in my face; you had every right to." Sarah swallowed hard. She didn't want to cry. "Especially after what happened to Rick and the hurt I caused him, but you didn't. I love you, Ma, and I will never do anything like that again."

Jo handed Richie to Becky before taking Sarah in her arms.

"Darling girl, you will always have a place in my family. You are my daughter. Nothing will ever change that. Rick loved you so much, and so do I. Now, please forget about the past. It is the future we have to look forward to. War or no war, this family is going to stick together, and when peace comes, we will all celebrate together."

"Here, here, Jo," shouted a number of the men. The women were in tears, even Becky, although she was doing her best to hide the fact. Sarah looked into Jo's face. "I hope Pa knew how much I loved him, although I didn't show it."

"He did, darling. Rick knew how you felt. He loved you so much. He would have done anything to see you back here, happy and healthy once more."

Happy? Was she? She guessed she was, although she was lonely. But the man of her dreams had made his choice. She had no option but to live with that decision. Walking Tall and his braves would come tomorrow; they may have some information on Bear. At least she would know he was well.

Sarah tied her hair up a couple of different ways, but it looked wrong.

"I will do it for you," Carrie said, having noticed her struggle. "Why are your hands shaking?"

Sarah met her sister's eyes in the mirror. Could she admit to how nervous she was about seeing Walking Tall and the other tribe members? Would they have news of Bear? Maybe he was living with an Indian maiden now.

"You love him, don't you? The Indian man who rescued you."

"Yes, Carrie, very much."

"Then you must tell him so. You deserve to find happiness, Sarah."

Sarah choked up at the look of love on her sister's face. Carrie didn't hold any grudge over Sarah running away. "Do you think that's true? After everything I put this family through?"

"Oh, Sarah, don't let the past ruin your future. You made mistakes, but so does everyone. Rick should never have discussed putting us in an orphanage in your hearing. You were a grieving child. Maybe we didn't need to tell know the truth about Pa, either. You shouldn't have run off with Edwin, but God knows how that hurt you. You need to live your life now. Jo wants you to be happy, and so do I."

Sarah stared at Carrie. Her little sister was all grown up.

"You love Stephen, don't you?"

Carrie turned scarlet as Sarah smiled at her.

"I thought that was a secret," the younger girl blurted out.

"Unless everyone is blind. It's obvious from the way you two look at each other." Sarah couldn't understand why nobody seemed to realize Carrie was madly in love with Jo's younger brother. Well, everyone apart from Bridget and Jo.

"You should just let it come out in the open. Stop trying to keep it a secret from Grandma Della."

"We were worried they wouldn't approve because of the age difference."

"He's not that much older than you. Anyway, it's not like you are the older one. Then they might raise their eyebrows," Sarah joked, making Carrie smile. "Jo thinks Grandma Della will approve."

"Does she? I have to go tell him. Thank you, Sarah. I am so glad you came back. Love you."

Sarah watched as Carrie ran off again. Her younger sister had always run everywhere. Sarah couldn't sit there much longer. She had to go downstairs and greet their guests. She had never thanked Walking Tall for sending Bear to find her and coming to rescue both of them.

She walked slowly down the stairs. The house was empty; the others must already be outside at the picnic. She knew Walking Tall wasn't keen on sitting inside the house. She had just reached the bottom step when the front door opened and in he walked. Bear looked even more handsome than in her dreams. His smile took her breath away.

"Hello, Sarah."

"Bear. What are you doing here? I thought you never came down from the mountain."

"I came to see you. Tala wanted to say hello."

She heard the dog whining at the door. Bear had left him outside. She opened the door, and the dog jumped almost into her arms, nearly knocking her over. He licked her all over, barking and running around her. She laughed at his antics. Then Bear held out his hand to help her stand up once more.

"I missed you."

She held her breath at the look in his eyes. Was it real, or was she hoping for too much? "Me too. You look good."

"Sarah, I have something to tell you."

At the serious look on his face, she closed her eyes. She didn't want to hear him tell her he had found another woman.

"Sarah, open your eyes. Please."

She opened them just in time to see him lean in to kiss her. The feel of his lips against hers was soft, like when a butterfly lands on your skin. He seemed to be waiting for a response from her. She moved into his arms, not letting his lips leave hers. It was all he needed as he swept her off her feet, deepening the kiss and making her heart sing.

He kissed her whole face before moving back to her lips.

"I love you. I have always loved you. Will you be my wife?"

She looked into his eyes, hardly believing what she was hearing. "Yes," she said, then she kissed him as hard as she could, trying to convince herself this was really happening and not another dream.

"If you could put my daughter down for a moment, perhaps she would introduce us?"

Bear dropped her suddenly, but at the last minute, he held onto her arm so she didn't fall over. She giggled at the look on his face as he stared at Jo. Jo was laughing, too.

"Bear, this is Jo, my ma. And Ma, this is Bear, the man I told you about."

"It is lovely to meet you in person. Thank you for looking after my daughter and returning her safely to us. Now, I take it you may be staying too?"

He couldn't move, couldn't speak. The woman was looking at him with such welcome and approval. An expression he had never seen before in a white woman's face.

"Funny, she didn't say you were mute," Jo teased as Sarah laughed.

"Ma, Bear asked me to marry him, and I said yes."

"I should hope so, dear. Only a husband should kiss his wife the way he was kissing you. Isn't that right, Bear?"

"Yes, ma'am." He finally found his voice.

"Oh, so you do speak?"

"Yes, ma'am." He smiled back at the woman before remembering he should have asked her permission before asking Sarah to marry him. "I would like your approval for our wedding."

"You have it, Bear, but I have one condition."

Bear looked at Sarah, but she was staring at Jo. He held Sarah's hand tightly as he looked back at Jo.

"I would like you to promise that wherever you two end up living, you will come back to visit us.

Having lost my daughter once, I do not wish to lose her again."

Relieved beyond measure, Bear smiled and shook Jo's hand. "Yes, ma'am. And thank you."

"No, thank you, Bear, for making my daughter's heart whole again. I wish you and her many years of happiness. Now excuse me. I have guests to attend to, and you two, well, maybe you should just get back to kissing."

Sarah giggled as Jo left them. Bear stared after her for a couple of seconds before turning back to Sarah.

"Your mother is an amazing woman."

"She is."

Sarah leaned in to kiss him again, but this time, her kiss was light.

"What is it?" he asked, knowing there was something bothering her.

"What made you change your mind? About being with me, I mean."

"Sarah, I always wanted to be with you. I just needed to be sure you wanted it, too. You had to see your family and put that behind you. I had to put my past behind me as well. Walking Tall was right; we both needed to forgive ourselves." He pulled her closer. "I love you with all my heart and soul. I will live wherever you wish."

"I will live with you. We can live with Walking Tall and his people."

"I do not think you are made for living in a teepee."

"I think you are right on that point, Bear. My sister is used to the finer things in life. I think you should build a house on some land Sarah owns. There is a nice spot by the river," Almanzo said as he walked in.

"Land? I don't own any land," Sarah said, looking at Almanzo. Bear could see from her face she was telling the truth.

"Rick left us all some land. You were to get it on your marriage. I think he wouldn't mind if you got it a little bit early so you could start building."

"Is this true, Almanzo, or are you trying to give us your land?"

"It is true. Rick wanted to always provide for you, even in his absence. What do you think, Bear? Could you deal with living this close to Sarah's family?"

Bear put his arm around Sarah's shoulders. "As long as my wife is happy, I can deal with anything."

"Good. Now come on outside. There are lots of people dying to meet you."

Bear took Sarah's hand, and together they walked outside.

EPILOGUE

THREE MONTHS LATER

The sun shining in the window woke Sarah up. Today was her wedding day. She couldn't wait to be married to Bear. She just hoped he would be back in time for the wedding. He'd told her he had something urgent to do before they got married and would be gone a week. Almanzo had also disappeared, saying he had to go to meet David. But David had returned home last night with lots of stories from Washington. No sign of Almanzo. Her brother wouldn't miss her big day. She just had to be patient.

A knock on her door alerted her before Bridget entered the room carrying a breakfast tray.

"Good morning love, how are you? I must say I don't see any sign of wedding nerves."

"Thank you for breakfast, Bridget. I can't wait to be Bear's wife. I would have married him the day he met you all for the first time, but he wanted to wait until our house was ready."

"Everyone did a wonderful job on that house. You are a lucky girl moving into such a nice home."

Sarah had been amazed at how fast her house was built. Bear had thought he would have to do all the work himself, but everyone had gathered to help him. Mr. and Mrs. Newland gave them a special price on a number of items for the interior of the house so they weren't starting off with a bare, empty dwelling.

Scott had given them a couple of horses to get their ranch going. Everyone had contributed something. They weren't rich, but they were comfortable.

"I know how lucky I am, Bridget, not just for the house or the land but for everyone's love. I am so happy I could burst."

"Glad to hear that. I would hate to have to tell everyone the wedding is off," Jo commented as she came into the room.

"Oh Ma. Where are the twins?"

"Downstairs, having their breakfast. They both want to put on their little dresses, but if they do, they won't be clean for the ceremony."

Sarah grinned, thinking of how excited Nancy and

Lena must be. She had asked them both to carry flowers for her. She wanted to make them part of her wedding.

"What time will the preacher call at?"

"He said about noon. It is a real pity you can't get married in town, but with feelings running high over the war, the reverend said it would be safer to get married here."

"I would rather get married here, anyway. I feel Rick is nearby. Does that sound silly?"

Jo kissed the top of her head. "No darling, it doesn't. I feel the same way."

Sarah coughed, trying to get control of her emotions. "Do you think the townsfolk will eventually accept Bear?"

"Some will and some won't. But either way, we do and that is all that counts. Bear will be so busy running the ranch and helping out with David's place, he won't know whether he is coming or going," Jo said, taking a cup of tea from Bridget's hands.

"He is wonderful with animals. They trust him." Sarah bit her lip, her appetite deserting her. Why wasn't he back yet? Had he changed his mind?

"Bear will be here. Sarah, trust your feelings. He loves you despite your faults as you do him. That is the start of a great marriage."

Sarah nodded, unable to speak for fear she would cry. Bear knew everything there was to know about her. He loved her. He would turn up, wouldn't he?

***

Bear hurried, knowing if they didn't make up the time, he would be late for his own wedding. Why hadn't he gone to collect Sarah's surprise sooner? He should have known something would happen to make him late. He closed his eyes, wishing he could tell Sarah he was coming. She knew he loved her, didn't she? She wouldn't think he had deserted her, would he?

"Walking Tall will be wondering where we are. We need to move faster."

"Never mind Walking Tall. My wife will kill me," Almanzo said, a frown on his face.

Bear looked at Almanzo and grinned. He had grown close to his wife's adopted brother over the last few months.

"Being late is not a good start to a wedding day." Grayhair, the brave Walking Tall had asked to accompany them, offered.

"I know that grouchy. But my wife will forgive me," Bear replied.

The brave didn't respond. Bear knew he didn't fully approve of his marriage. Not all of Walking Tall's braves agreed with the close relationship their leader had with the whites. Paco, Walking Tall's father and a great Chief had always held the opinion that every man, regardless of the color of their skin, deserved a chance. Walking Tall continued that belief. Grayhair, despite his name, was young. He was from another tribe, but Walking Tall had offered him a home when that tribe was moved to the reservation. Bear wondered if it had been a mistake to let the Brave accompany him. But it was too late for regrets now.

Almanzo burst into a gallop, causing Grayhair to look after him.

"My house is on the other side of this river, about two miles away. We will get there shortly. Follow me," Bear explained.

Bear pushed his horse, who seemed to recognize he was nearly home. Tala barked with joy as he rushed ahead of Bear. The dog's barking brought the guests out in to the sunshine looking at them. Bear searched the faces, but there was no sign of Sarah. Scott stepped forward to hold his horse as he dismounted. "Where is Sarah?"

"You are almost three hours late. What kept you?" Scott hissed.

"Bear will explain. I need to find my wife."

Almanzo answered.

"I know I am late. I am sorry, but I had something important to do. Find Sarah please."

Sarah came running even as he asked Scott to find her.

"Bear, you are here? I thought something had happened to you. Oh thank God you are safe."

He nearly lost balance as she flung herself into his arms, tears streaming down her face. Surely she hadn't thought he'd deserted her? Hadn't she learned to put her past behind her?

"Sarah, I am sorry I was late, but I had a little bit of trouble finding your present."

"My present?"

"Well, you can't give another person as a present, but I thought you might like an extra guest at our wedding. He took a bit of persuading."

"Who?"

Bear stood back and pushed Johnny forward. Sarah went white, then red, before reaching for the boy.

"Johnny. How glad I am to see you. You have grown so much."

Bear hid a grin. His wife to be was a bad liar. The boy had grown in height, but he was skin and bone, slowly starving to death. He must have worked all hours in the mine.

"That man kidnapped me and then the Indian said

I had to come. I don't know why you want me here." Johnny looked at the ground sullenly, making Sarah want to pull the seven-year-old close, but she had to move carefully.

"Almanzo, you were part of this surprise? Thank you."

Almanzo bowed before wrapping his arm around Tilly's shoulders. "Bear knew where the town was and the name of the boy, but for obvious reasons, he couldn't go near the village to look for him. It took some persuading to get him to come with us."

"Johnny, I am so glad you came. I wanted to say I was sorry. For not helping your ma. I behaved very selfishly that night. I had my reasons, but I always wondered how you were."

"I am fine." Johnny looked around him, at the tables, groaning with food in particular. "This is a nice place. No idea why you came to Tyrell's pit?"

"Neither do I, Johnny, but I was a different girl back then. At least I met Bear, and you. That made it worth it."

Johnny didn't look too convinced. Sarah looked from the boy to the man who would become her husband. Bear nodded, a wide smile on his face.

"Johnny, would you like to come and live here? We could use a hand around the place. We are going to rear horses for the army. We need a strong man. "

"Depends on what you are paying," the boy said, obviously pretending to be disinterested, but Sarah had seen the spark in his eyes.

The adults grinned at the words coming from the seven-year-old boy.

"How about three good meals a day and a roof over your head? A nice bed of your own. Maybe some friends to play with when the chores are done. Would that work?"

Johnny spat on his hand and held it out to Sarah. "Deal." Sarah giggled before picking Johnny up and spinning him around. "Right, young man, your first job is to accompany my little sisters to my wedding."

"Can I have something to eat first?" Johnny asked, hope written all over his face. "Girls are hard work."

"No, you can't, young man. The Reverend has been waiting long enough. Come along everyone."

Jo shepherded the family over to the apple trees. This was where the ceremony would be held.

* * *

Bear reached for Sarah and together they made their way towards the gathering.

"I am sorry I was late."

"You're forgiven. I can't believe you and Almanzo worked together to bring Johnny here."

"Why not? We both love you." Bear kissed Sarah soundly. "I know how much you regret not helping his ma. At least now, maybe we can put all the regrets behind us."

Sarah blinked rapidly. He guessed to keep the tears at bay. He kissed her gently on each eye, trying to show her how much he loved her.

Then he took her hand and together they walked to the Preacher and said their vows. Whatever the future brought, they were no longer alone.

* * *

Thank you so much for reading the five books in Trails of Heart. Please enjoy this sneak peek into the bestselling Orphan Train Series.

Orphan Train Escape

New York 1893, Carmel's Mission

Lily Doherty sang softly as she moved through the rooms of the sanctuary. It had taken the best part of five years to get Carmel's Mission, the sanctuary named after her husband's grandmother, working as she hoped. Initially, her project had been met by skepticism. So many New Yorkers believed the poor chose to live in poverty and decay. But she had persevered.

With her husband, Charlie, and Mr. Prentice—Mr. P as she liked to call him—behind her, she hadn't let any setback stop her from moving forward. Dr. Elmwood had also been a huge asset, helping the ladies and children with medical issues free of charge.

Finally, things began to change. Word spread among the people she most wanted to reach, that the help she offered didn't come with many conditions. She didn't require them to change religions or start attending church in order to be helped. She didn't impose her beliefs on anyone. Yes, she had Father Nelson and Pastor Adams working with her. Both men were similar and believed being a Christian meant you helped all those in need not just those you considered worthy. Of course, their hope was always that others would see their way of life as the best way and follow suit. It worked, too, as both men saw an increase in attendances at their respective services.

Many members of the local community had got behind her idea and had offered their help as well, not only in money but also in labor. They were the people who touched her heart more. The men and women who had toiled all week long but still gave the sanctuary an hour or so. The women cleaned the rooms and made the large pots of soup she distributed to those in need, as well as the residents of the sanctuary. Lily hoped it would continue, although the numbers requiring her help were rising. She was particularly concerned about the number of children living on the streets. Something more had to be done for them.

Charlie was worried about the economy. He had his head stuck in the New York Times again this morning. Where had the happy-go-lucky lad she had married gone? Smiling, she admitted to herself they had both grown in the last five years. Their marriage was a joy to both of them; their respective work a blessing. Charlie helped with legal issues as and when they arose. His employer, a man he had saved in the great whiteout of '88, had recognized Charlie's strengths and his position with the firm was rock solid.

She tried to be more positive about the economy, although she had to admit it was scary hearing about the next bank closing. Mr. P also seemed more on edge than usual. And the news from her friends back in Clover Springs, Colorado was heartbreaking. Both Erin and Ellen had written about the number of miners finding their way to the town, their jobs gone overnight. The price of silver had dropped drastically and was still moving downward.

Her office door opened, admitting a matronly lady. Lily smiled at the woman, who worked almost as hard as she did.

"Good morning, Lily. Lovely day, isn't it?" Mrs. Wilson's smile could light up a room.

"It is indeed, Mrs. Wilson. How are the ladies?"

"Doing much better now you've secured more work for them. They were scared you would send them back onto the streets."

The news about the economy always hit the poor worst of all, as they were the ones to pay a heavier price. When you lived day to day, never having sufficient money to meet all your bills, any reduction in earnings would be devastating.

"You know I would never do that." She prayed to God she'd never have to. But if the economy did spiral downwards, would she have enough to keep the Sanctuary going?

"I know Lily, but you have to remember, not all of them know you like I do. They don't know you were once as poor as they are. They wouldn't believe me if I told them about your past. You are very much a lady now."

Lily grinned as she looked at her clothes. If you judged her solely on the way she was dressed, it was obvious she was financially secure. Her dress, while modest in fashion, was made of the highest quality cotton. Her hands were lily-white and not red raw, like many of the women in the soup lines. She was lucky.

She'd left a horrible past behind with the help of Doc Erin and Mick Quinn from Clover Springs. They had brought her to New York, where she met Mr. P. Their visit coincided with the biggest tragedy to hit New York. Lily shivered, remembering how many had died during the '88 blizzard. Was it really five years ago?

CHAPTER 47

Bridget Collins pushed the lank hair out of her eyes as she stretched her back. Everything ached from her head to her toes and it wasn't yet midday. She could only imagine how bad it was for the older women who worked here. She was supposed to be in her prime – yet at nineteen she felt every year of her age and a hundred more.

Oaks Laundry, where she worked, was situated in the basement of a tenement building where fresh air was the stuff of daydreams. She wished she could take a break, but her supervisor, Mr. Webster, was even more on edge than usual. Mr. Oaks senior, the owner, must be on site. He was strict, although she preferred him to his son. The way young Mr. Oaks looked at her made her want to crawl out of her own skin.

She pushed the shirts back into the water, having

scrubbed the cuffs and collars with the harsh lye soap. Her thoughts drifted back to her childhood in Ireland, like the green, open fields she had run through with her brothers and sisters on their way to school. Mam had insisted her children would do better by learning to read and write. Only a proper education gave the poor a chance in life. Poor mam. Bridget never thought she would be glad her mam was dead. But it would have killed her to see how her children were faring. Coming to America had been her mam's dream. She believed in the stories sent back to Ireland from people who had emigrated. This was supposed to be the land of opportunity. Bridget sighed, wondering how people had written home such tales of hope when the reality was so different.

Maura, her eldest sister was at home, her heart grieving for her fiancé, killed in the explosion at their work last weekend. In the space of two days, she had lost not only her job, but her hope for the future. David had idolized Maura, calling her his older woman – he'd been twenty to Maura's twenty-two. He had protected the whole family against the worst of tenement life. Bridget squeezed her eyes shut to stop a tear escaping. She could still see David now, his big blue eyes lit up from inside. He was always smiling. How come the good died young? Her brothers, Shane, and Michael, were running wild. She suspected they were involved with one of the many gangs who preyed on the poor. Kathleen, her favorite sister, was slowly going blind sewing button holes. Liam, the youngest boy, was out collecting rags as he tried to provide for the family at six years of age. He was particularly close to Annie, his junior by two years, and couldn't bear to see her go hungry. What would they do?

* * *

"Good afternoon Bridget, you look mighty pretty today."

Bridget stilled, her backbone going rigid at the sound of his voice. She hadn't seen him come in, so he'd caught her by surprise. Pretty? Covered in sweat with lank hair and red, raw hands? He needed his eyes tested.

"Good afternoon, sir." Her tone was as polite as she could make it without being servile. Yes, he was the son of the boss, but that didn't make him her better. Mam said the goodness of one's heart was the value of a man, not how much money he kept in the bank.

"I need to see you in the office," Mr. Oaks said. "There has been a complaint."

As soon as he walked away, confident she would follow, she wilted. What type of complaint had there been this time? She was sick of his attempts to get her alone. How many times did she have to tell him she was a good, Catholic girl? What he wanted from her was for her husband alone. She pulled the tub away from the heat and, wiping her stinging hands on her apron, walked slowly to the office.

She could feel the eyes on her back, although anyone checking on the women would think they hadn't stopped working. The tension in the air was palpable. Those who had worked for Oaks Laundry and Sewing for years knew what being summoned to the office meant. For the men, it was bad news. For the women, the younger ones anyway, it was a lot worse. She saw a couple of the women cross themselves and hoped they had shared a prayer for her as well. She pushed her shoulders back. Whatever he threatened her with this time, she still wasn't going to give in to him. Never.

"There you are," he said as she entered his office. "The walk across the floor seems to take you longer each time, Bridget."

She ignored the reprimand but stood with her hands balled at her sides, her fingernails hurting the insides of her palms. His grey blue eyes, almost colorless, were fixated on her chest as he addressed her. She glanced at his suit, the golden chain from his watch hanging from the pocket of his waistcoat another reminder of how wealthy he was. She glanced at his face momentarily, thinking of the comments someone from the factory floor had made about him wishing to model his appearance on the Prince of Wales. She had never seen a picture of the Prince but wondered if his wife thought a full beard and long whiskers to be attractive. It certainly didn't suit Mr. Oaks making him look even uglier than his behavior.

The office door closed behind her, shutting off most of the noise of the shop floor. The air in the office would have been sweeter than that of the laundry but for his presence. There was a pervading sense of evil about him, something she couldn't explain in words.

She refused to look him in the eye. Instead, she stared at a point above his head.

"Why don't you sit down Bridget and have some soup. It's delicious."

The smell of the soup stirred her stomach. She hoped it wouldn't start grumbling. She didn't want the man to know how hungry she was. But if he thought she was going to sell herself for some food, he was wrong. It was time to try to take a little control back. She was an employee, not his servant. Or at least it was supposed to be that way.

"You mentioned a complaint, sir."

"Yes, but not against you, Bridget. Your work is always to the highest standard."

What was she doing in his office then? He hadn't said her work was of high quality when she got demoted from the sewing department to the laundry. But she kept her mouth shut and waited. He had something on his mind; she could tell by the tone of his voice. He was baiting her. To him, she wasn't a person, but a plaything. Something to amuse himself with when he got bored. And she wasn't the first.

When she started in the laundry, the girl called to the office on several occasions was Mary Rourke. Mary, who ended up in the Hudson River, her swelling abdomen evidence of her so-called crime. Poor Mary. She'd been desperate. This evil man had told her she had to pay for her father's mistakes. The same father who had thrown his own daughter out when the evidence of what she had done came to light.

But Bridget wasn't Mary.

"You aren't curious about why you are in here?" he asked.

"I expect you will tell me, sir."

She had to be careful. Her temper was rising, and it could easily cost Bridget her job. Her pay wasn't much, but it was enough to keep the roof over their heads when combined with what Kathleen earned. They depended on what young Liam earned from rag picking to supplement the cost of food.

"A girl in the sewing section…"

Her heart thumped when he didn't complete his sentence. She could feel his eyes boring into her body. She knew he was talking about Kathleen, but she was a good girl. She wouldn't give cause for complaint unless someone had done something to her.

"If you have touched her, you—" she spat.

"Bridget Collins, remember yourself. You know I wouldn't put a finger on such an insipid creature. I prefer my women to have fire in their bellies. Makes for a much more satisfying arrangement if you catch my drift."

He wasn't exactly subtle. Of course, she understood him.

"But as the complaint was made, we had no choice but to send your sister home. Her position has already been filled."

Her stomach dropped at the same time as her heart started beating faster. He'd fired Kathleen. Now, at a time when jobs were like gold dust. Her family couldn't survive without Kathleen's wages. But then he would know that. He was using the situation to remind her he held complete power over her future and that of her siblings. Her fingernails dug deeper into her palms.

"Don't you have something to say?" he asked.

"No, sir." She wasn't going to apologize. Kathleen hadn't done anything wrong, she was sure of it. The sixteen-year-old girl was too shy and afraid of her own shadow to cause trouble. Mam used to say Kathleen was born with a heart too sensitive for this world.

He moved closer to her, blocking her exit. She stepped away from him until the office table prevented her escape.

He pushed a strand of hair away from her face while she held her body rigid, so it wouldn't flinch. She wasn't going to show him any fear. He delighted in making people fear him.

"Now, tell me Bridget, how will we make this situation work? I have been told to fire you as well. We have to make an example, to show the other workers that laziness and poor workmanship will not be tolerated."

She stared over his shoulder, refusing to rise to his tricks. They both knew there wasn't a lazy bone in her sister's body. But protesting that wouldn't change anything.

He moved so close it was almost as if the only thing separating them were their clothes. She could feel his breath on her neck, his expensive cologne making her nostrils sting.

"Bridget, we could have so much fun together. You wouldn't go hungry. You might be able to afford a nicer home. Your brothers wouldn't be in danger of being locked up."

She couldn't help flinching. What did he know of Michael and Shane?

"Yes, I know your brothers. In fact, I may have mentioned my concerns to a couple of friends on the force. They can't be allowed to prey on the poor. Making people's lives miserable with their thieving, drinking, and debauchery."

If she had been anywhere else, she may have been amused by the irony of this man using those terms about someone else. Isn't that what he did every day? He may not steal in the conventional sense, but keeping his workers locked in this basement for twelve hours a day and paying them a pitiful wage was a different form of stealing, wasn't it?

"You will have to be very nice to me, Bridget. I hold the power to destroy your little family. Although it would pain me, believe me, I will do it."

"Pain you? Nothing could make you feel anything with a heart of iron. You won't get anything from me, Stephen Oaks. I told you before, and I will tell you again. My body isn't for sale, not at any price."

He grinned, making her stomach roil. "Now we both know that isn't true. Every woman has her price. For women of my class, it's marriage and a suitable home. In return, they know they have to fulfil their duty. For women of your class, some good food usually is enough for them to—"

"Not me. I was brought up better than that. Now do your worst, but you won't have me."

He trailed his lips along her neck, leaving her skin wet as he gripped her arms savagely.

"Believe me I will. I always get what I want."

Desperate, Bridget's hands flew behind her. There must be something on the desk she could use to defend herself. His grip on her tightened as his lips moved all over her face. She refused to let him kiss her, causing him to call her a horrible word. He pushed himself against her. Time was running out. Her fingers grabbed wildly on the desk, finally finding something sharp. A letter opener. She grabbed it without thinking and slashed at him. The element of surprise was on her side. Her aim was off, but she still managed to slice his ear. His blood dripped over her hand just as he cried out and moved slightly away, his focus on his injury. She pushed him farther and ran to the door. Opening it, she flew from the office and didn't stop until she was halfway home. What had she done? He was bound to report her and then what would happen to her family? She picked up her skirts and fled home, back to the tenement building.

CHAPTER 48

"Bridget, what happened? Kathleen came home and went to bed without a word," Bridget's eldest sister, Maura, said.

Bridget didn't stop as she stepped inside their room in the tenement. She didn't even close the door behind her in her usual attempt to block out the disgusting stench.

"Maura, pack up everything," she said, fighting to remain calm. "We have to get out of here now."

"But why? Where will we go?" Maura whined.

"I don't know, but the police will be here soon. They will put the children in the asylum and…. Oh Maura, I'll tell you later but please get ready. We don't have much time." Bridget saw Kathleen get out of bed and dress quickly. She sent her white-faced sister out to find Liam and Annie.

"Where will we go?" Maura repeated, standing still as if they had all the time in the world. "This is our home."

Bridget glanced around the windowless room that had sheltered them for the last three years ever since daddy had lost his job on the railways. Kathleen had covered the biggest cracks with newspaper in an effort to make the hovel homelier. The newspapers didn't keep out any of the sounds around them. The rat's claws scraping against the plaster, their high-pitched squeaks as they fought each other for dominance. She didn't know which was worse, the noise of the rats, the drunken neighbors singing bawdy sounds, or the noisy lovemaking that seemed to follow.

It was impossible to know how many people lived in these tenements. The multistory brick building had been built years before for far grander purposes and certainly wasn't designed to hold so many immigrants. Now, each room was tenanted, sometimes by more than one family. Bridget knew they had been lucky not being forced to share their room with strangers.

Lucky? If daddy hadn't fallen foul of the landlord, wrongly accused of a crime, their lives would have been so much better in Ireland. They had been poor but happy. The air had been fresh and there was more room to move around. If she closed her eyes, she could see her mam spinning wool in the evening, exchanging a warm smile with their daddy sitting by the fire. Bridget's mam had been a powerhouse of energy, by day working as a seamstress in the big house, and in her spare time, she had raised chickens, selling the eggs at the local store. Sometimes she sold cheese and brown bread at the market. Now Mam and Daddy were dead and all they had left was each other.

Bridget reined in her impatience with her sister. Maura was the eldest, but she was behaving worse than Annie, her four-year-old sister.

Thankfully, Bridget had thought about where they should go on her run back home. They would go to Father Nelson at the church. He would help them. He had to. He'd believe she was only protecting herself, wouldn't he? He wasn't like the previous priest. He was different. She had to take a chance on him. It was their only option. They certainly couldn't stay here, just waiting to be picked up.

"Where are Michael and Shane?" she asked her sister.

"Out, as always." Maura's resigned reply spoke volumes as she poked at the fire. Maura had started dinner, lighting a small fire on the paving stones in the corner of the room. The smoke made everyone's eyes water, but it was the only way to cook the potatoes which were baking in the embers. Maura had done all the cooking since David had died. It was all she did. The boys ran wild but, in fairness, even David hadn't managed to control the boys. They were old enough to fend for themselves, being fifteen and seventeen.

"We can't wait for them. I'll send Colm Fleming to find them and tell them not to come back here but to head straight for the church. Mrs. Fleming may use the room—we've paid for the next two weeks." Bridget looked around the small room they used as a bedroom, kitchen, and everything else. If only she hadn't met the rent collector last evening. She would have that money to tide them over. But she couldn't live by "if only." It raised more questions than it answered.

"Oh Bridget, I can't believe this. David was so sure things were turning around for us and now it's all gone wrong. I just can't do it, I can't..."

Bridget watched in horror as her elder sister descended into a fit of screaming.

She slapped Maura hard on the face. "Pull yourself together. You are the eldest, not me. Mam depended on us to protect the young ones."

Maura stared at her resentfully, but she didn't say a word. Instead she took the potatoes out of the fire and threw clay on the embers to put it out.

Bridget packed up their pitiful belongings and, within fifteen minutes of Bridget coming home, the room was empty. Kathleen came back with the younger children, all remained tight-lipped as they looked from Bridget and Maura to the bags at their feet.

"We have to go see Father Nelson about a new home. It's time for a change," Bridget said, trying to inject some enthusiasm into her voice. She didn't want to scare the young 'uns.

"I like it here. Mrs. Fleming is nice to us. Why do we have to leave?" Liam asked, his hand in Annie's. The little girl sucked her other thumb, her eyes wide with fear. Bridget's heart clenched with hate for Mr. Oaks and his like. This was the only home the children remembered and now they were losing that too.

"Don't worry Liam. The next house will be nicer. I promise." She crossed her fingers hoping she would be proved right. Looking over the child's head at the dirty, damp walls, it wouldn't take much to find somewhere nicer to live.

Mrs. Fleming wished them well, hugging all of them as she dabbed at her eyes with her apron. "Don't you worry about nothing, darlings. I will tell them fellas you went to family in Jersey. By the time they chase after that goose, you will have flown. May God have mercy on their souls as straight to the devil they will go for preying on such lovely girls as youse. Thank God your poor mam is dead and buried."

***

They trudged through the streets. Nobody commented on their sorry little procession, too wrapped up in their own survival.

Father Nelson was in the church when they arrived. Bridget told him the full story of what had happened, watching his facial expressions closely. At one point he looked so furious she took a step back from him.

"Bridget Collins," he said. "Never be afraid of standing up for yourself. You are not to blame. If I wasn't a man of God, I would…well, the least said about that the better. Let's go and see what my lovely housekeeper can rustle up for you. A full belly will make you all feel better."

"Father, what if the police come here?"

"You let me worry about that, young Bridget. I have some very good friends on the force myself. The man you are running from isn't the only one with connections. Come on, child, take that look off your face. You are all safe here."

Bridget wanted to believe him, but she couldn't. She knew how it worked. The rich always won.

But her younger siblings didn't need to know how she felt. She forced a smile on her face and gathered them together as they followed the priest into his house. His housekeeper's reception wasn't as warm. She stared at them. Looking through her eyes, Bridget could see the reason for her distaste. They were all filthy, and the younger one's heads were crawling. But what could they do? There was no running water in the hovel they called home, never mind soap. Bridget pushed her hair back. They had done their best.

"Mrs. Riordan, these poor children are running from evil. They need our help. A decent meal followed by a hot bath and a good scrub is what's in order. You provide the meal and we will look after everything else later."

"Yes, Father Nelson."

"Now, I need to go out. I shall return shortly. Bridget, could you come with me please?"

Torn between wanting to stay with her siblings and doing what the priest asked, Bridget hesitated. Maura wasn't being particularly helpful, but even she wouldn't let any harm come to the children. Would she? Father Nelson misinterpreted her reluctance to go with him. He assumed she was hungry.

"Have some food first and then we will go together.

Your family will be safe here. Mrs. Riordan may not smile much but sure the woman has a heart of gold," Father Nelson whispered. Bridget looked at the housekeeper and hoped he was right.

Maybe the lady was someone who found it hard to show her feelings.

To read more, click Here

CHARACTER LIST

Hughes Homestead

Rick Hughes (deceased)
Jo Hughes nee Thompson - his wife
Nancy & Lena Hughes - their six year old twins
Adopted three trail orphans
Sarah Hughes - 18 - Rick's niece eloped with Edwin Morgan
Carrie Hughes - 14 - Rick's niece
Almanzo Price - 18 now married to Tilly
Bridget Murphy - housekeeper

Jones Homestead

Scott Jones (former Boss of Wagon Train – Indian name He Who Runs)
Becky Jones nee Thompson - his wife
Jake and Ruth - six year old twins

CHARACTER LIST

Nathan and Annie - three year old twins
Willie – six months old

Clarke Homestead
David Clarke
Eva Clarke nee Thompson - his wife
Patrick known as Pat - 7 1/2 years
Samuel known as Sam - 4 1/2 years

Thompson Homestead
Paddy Thompson
Della Thompson, his wife

Indians
Walking Tall
Mia – Almanzo's half sister.

ACKNOWLEDGMENTS

This book wouldn't have been possible without the help of so many people. Thanks to Erin Dameron-Hill for my fantastic covers. Erin is a gifted artist who makes my characters come to life.

I have an amazing editors. But sometimes errors slip through. I am very grateful to the ladies from my readers group who volunteered to proofread my book. Special thanks go to Marlene, Cindy, Meisje , Judith, Janet, Tamara, Cindi, Nethanja and Denise who all spotted errors (mine) that had slipped through.

Please join my Facebook group for readers of Historical fiction. Come join us for games, prizes, exclusive content, and first looks at my latest releases. Rachel's readers group

Last, but by no means least, huge thanks and love to my husband and my three children.

ALSO BY RACHEL WESSON

The Resistance Sisters

Darkness Falls

Light Rises

Hearts at War

When's Mummy Coming

A Mother's Promise

WWII Stand Alone

Stolen from her Mother

Song of Courage

Orphans of Hope House

Home for unloved Orphans (Orphans of Hope House 1)

Baby on the Doorstep (Orphans of Hope House 2)

Women and War

Gracie under Fire

Penny's Secret Mission

Molly's Flight

Hearts on the Rails

Orphan Train Escape

Orphan Train Trials

Orphan Train Christmas

Orphan Train Tragedy

Orphan Train Strike

Orphan Train Disaster

Orphan Train Memories

Trail of Hearts - Oregon Trail Series

Oregon Bound (book 1)

Oregon Dreams (book 2)

Oregon Destiny (book 3)

Oregon Discovery (book 4)

Oregon Disaster (book 5)

12 Days of Christmas - co -authored series.

The Maid - book 8

Clover Springs Mail Order Brides

Katie (Book 1)

Mary (Book 2)

Sorcha (Book 3)

Emer (Book 4)

Laura (Book 5)

Ellen (Book 6)

Thanksgiving in Clover Springs (book 7)

Christmas in Clover Springs (book8)

Erin (Book 9)

Eleanor (book 10)

Cathy (book 11)

Mrs. Grey

Clover Springs East

New York Bound (book 1)

New York Storm (book 2)

New York Hope (book 3)

Printed in Great Britain
by Amazon

46211187R00162